THE MIND-RIDERS

Borgo Press Books by BRIAN STABLEFORD

THE MIND-RIDERS

A SCIENCE FICTION NOVEL

BRIAN STABLEFORD

THE BORGO PRESS
MMXII

THE MIND-RIDERS

FIRST BORGO PRESS EDITION

Published by Wildside Press LLC

www.wildsidebooks.com

THE MIND-RIDERS

CONTENTS

CHAPTER ONE

It was late when I left the studio, and I'd missed the worst of the crowds. I'd also missed the worst of the afternoon stink because the sun was low and there were clouds blowing from the east. Around noon it had been hot enough to cook the garbage in the alleys, but it was cool now and the flies were settling down.

I walked to the monorail station with my hands in my pockets and my eyes fixed on the ground about ten feet in front of where I was walking. It hadn't been a great day, and I wasn't feeling like looking the world in the face. At long last, though, we'd put the knights-in-armor thing to bed. The feelers could move in on Monday and the techs could cut the tape inch by inch into consumer packages. Our part was done, and I had seen the last of all the fancy tinfoil for a good long while. The producer was due for another stroke of self-declared genius, but the one thing you could say for him was that he was inconsistent. Whatever he came up with would be a change.

Personally, I didn't even believe that the travesty we'd just done would ever reach the public. Network might have no taste but they were sensitive as hell about clumsy E-tapes, and no matter how hard the feelers worked they'd never make those tinclad idiots seem remotely human. It was all too absurd.

So much for chivalry.

When I got to the station there were ten minutes or so to wait. Twenty or thirty other people were there—almost all Network staff of some sort. They looked bored and tired, and stared at the tracks or the down line platform with a uniform glassiness. Even the ones that were talking didn't look at one another. The whole scene was completely enervated. It would never be allowed to happen inside a sim. Simulation is far more alive than life.

I nodded to a couple of techs who worked along with me, on and off. They nodded back and didn't smile. Keyboard staff spend so much of their time enveloped by the miracle of MiMaC that they no longer know how to communicate with one another. They take off their headsets and switch themselves off right along with their machines.

But there was one man in the loose knot who saw me and who moved over to stand close to me. His name was Jimmy Schell, and he'd recently moved in across the corridor from me in stack 232. He had a job with Network as a feeler, but they were still testing him out.

He was excited, which meant he'd dubbed a tape.

"I thought you'd've gone," he said, without bothering to say hello. He presumed a lot on the fact that we were neighbors, but he was new into cap living and probably hadn't cottoned on to the disposability of neighbor relations. The turnover is fast.

"Wrapping up King Arthur," I muttered, leaving nothing in my tone to suggest that I might welcome his following up that particular line of conversation. I needn't have bothered. He didn't want to talk about me.

He opened his mouth to say something, as if he were in a hell of a rush to pour the words out, but nothing emerged. Jimmy had a stammer—not the kind of stammer which makes you repeat letters or syllables, but the kind which catches you up as you try to form a sound and stops you dead while your face goes red and you look like constipation is killing you. His mind seemed to be prone to the same kind of jamming from time to time. He didn't live on his thinking. That's what made him into a potential feeler. Feelers mustn't think—it gets in the way.

"—Got a job," he forced out at last, the G bursting like a little bomb and all the other sounds lurching as they toppled.

"In the can?" I said, fairly pleasantly—fairly pleased, come to that. I was glad to see the kid getting himself up off the ground. Six months and he could be a household name. I wasn't likely to do any handling for him, but I could well be playing opposite.

He was nodding vigorously. "On the Net," he said. "Next week."

"Commercial?" I asked, trying not to let it sound like a dirty word.

"Beer," he said. "On a beach. They had me in the sweatbox for—*hours*. God, it tasted good!"

"It would," I said.

His face clouded slightly, though I hadn't meant to sound cynical.

"You think—" he began. He had to stop. He didn't know what I thought.

I shook my head. "It's work," I said. "It'll show what you can do. Everybody begins the same way."

They have to. Commercials live on naïveté even more than the plastic drama. It takes quite some simplicity of mind to be able to generate wild enthusiasm over some bland crud. It takes a kid who *needs* to feel good—can't get through the day without it.

The people know it's fake even when it's honest, of course. They know that sun-bronzed Apollo pouncing about the beach is being puppeted by a bored handler while some callow kid radiates his glamour. But if it's good, if it feels *right*, they play the game. They go out and buy the crud. They buy the plastic drama too. It isn't real but it's comfortable. It feels okay. Some even prefer it that way—they like the pap and can't take it straight. Even the addicts of the authentic adrenalin high don't live on an undiluted diet—it would blow their E-sodden minds.

So Jimmy was doing a real public service. Keeping the wheels of modern life in motion. He'd be a hit, I was sure. Up like a shooting star. And, by the same token, burned out as fast. Fame kills feelers. It dispels the simplicity of mind, the *gaucherie*, which is so essential to their ability to radiate good feelings.

The train came in and I stepped forward reflexively, short-circuiting Jimmy's next remark even better than his stammer could have. I elbowed my way in through the sliding doors with practiced ease, trying to beat the comptechs to the seats, but it was no good. Standing room only. It wasn't *that* late.

I grabbed a strap and hung hard, making the tendons in my wrist go rigid. As the train accelerated I was thrown back, then had to lean into the movement. Starting like that made some people sick but the monorail had a schedule to keep up, and even these days the trains ran on time. They really used their speed between stops.

There's always a big demand for speed between stops.

Jimmy was behind me, and once we were under way I edged round to face him. He was looking at me as if he expected something. Congratulations, maybe. Or a funny story.

Anything to keep the word-flow going.

I grinned at him.

"I think I did it good," he said, confidentially.

"Sure," I said, nodding. "They give you a hard time?"

"No. I think they liked it. I didn't have to go back in the— *box.*"

A thirst is a thirst. It wasn't that they were paying him for, though they'd sweat him up to get it. They were paying him for *gladness,* for *pleasure,* for *relief*—all the things that go into feeling how wonderful a can of beer can be. That's what they'd be sending out good and strong over the beach scene.

"You know," he said, "I thought they'd need lots of—*people* for a thing like that. But only the guy is real. The rest—" He tailed off, not because his glitch had caught up with him but because he realized he didn't have to tell me. I'd been in the studio since he was an infant.

"The girl doesn't need a handler," I told him. "She's what they call a visual cue. She isn't called upon to move, let alone feel—she just has to be there. The crowds in the fringes—well, they're just phantoms. Just an illusion—a flicker in the walls of the sim. There's a general-purpose procedure in the computer to make crowds. They're just something that has to be vaguely sketched in. Nobody pays them any real attention—they're always in the background, mentally as well as physically."

There was a short pause. Then, in a neutral voice, he said, "You don't handle commercials." There was a question implied, but he wasn't sure enough of himself to ask.

I shook my head. "It's not my bag," I said. "I was never into moving suggestively. The body language I talk is made of rougher stuff. I did some heroes when the fashion was for tough parts, but mostly I do bad boys and spares."

Spares are characters which aren't B-linked. They act in the sim but the characters aren't made available to the vampires so there's no feeler dubbed in over the action. I can move a sim as well as anyone, but body language is important—a feeler needs a lot of help from his handler, lest the vamp-appeal and the ratings should ever-so-slightly decline. My movements don't talk feeler language, so I generally get the villain or the mug to hustle around. I don't mind. Who wants to be a plastic hero?

"You're good," said Jimmy, tentatively.

"How d'you know?" I asked. Handlers don't get their names on the credit reels.

"I know some of the stuff you did," he said. "I looked it up in records. Some of the shows I used to like best when I was—" This time he gave up, maybe figuring that I could complete the sentence on my own.

"Why?" I asked. "You want to find out who was living across the way?" I tried not to sound sour about it.

He nodded, knowing somehow that the words just weren't going to come for a moment or two. I let silence settle.

My eyes lingered on Jimmy's face for just a few seconds before being driven away by embarrassment. It looked like a curious kind of mask. It was the face of a small child blown up to size and pasted on to an adult frame. Jimmy wasn't tall but he was stocky and solidly built—not the kind of guy an anemic mugger would single out as a natural victim. His wide eyes and his little nose and his all-around cuteness looked slightly grotesque on a body built for wielding a sledgehammer.

I let my gaze lurch drunkenly to the window, passing over the dull, vacuous creatures who filled the carriage with a faintly offensive aroma of acrylic plastic and cheap deodorant. They wore with absent-minded unanimity the expression of utter boredom, of transit between phases in their lives. They were in the process of translation from context A (work) to context B (home) and they had no script to govern the intermission. It had never occurred to them that these were minutes like any other minutes, to be lived. To them, it was a time to be endured, a time to be waited out with all senses switched off. They sat in suspended animation, their eyes—like mine—extending to stare at the blurred world dragged across the window-frames at two hundred KPH. I couldn't figure out what made me any different, but I always had the idea haunting me that I ought to be.

At that kind of speed, there's nothing solid outside the train. Everything beyond the traveling microcosm becomes liquid, unable to linger long enough on-the retina to form a hard image. At two hundred KPH the world is ultra-soft, dissolving into chaos. The sun flashes from a billion windows, and there seems to be a glittering sea outside, immune from action and change.

Time, someone used to say, is for spending, not for saving. Or for killing. But today's people are mean with their time. They can't pile it up in banks or nursery-rhyme counting-houses but they can staunch its flow, forcing it to clot before they pick the scab and let it go again.

Sometimes I wonder how the hell they think they're ever going to collect the interest on their savings.

"Who do you think will win the fight?" said Jimmy, finding his voice and cutting into my thoughts with it.

I froze slightly. It was a bad question. But he wasn't to know that.

"Herrera," I said, clipping the syllables.

"They say Angeli is hot," he said, rejoicing in the way he was getting his sentences out and failing to pick up the hint.

"Herrera will win," I said.

He must have caught the inflection that time. He knew he'd somehow hit a nerve.

"You going to watch the—*fight*?" A fatuous question, hardly worth the agony of the stammer.

"Aren't we all?" I replied.

"Plugged into Herrera?" he said, not stopping himself in time. It was an indelicate question. Not the kind of thing you ask in mixed company. He realized, too late, and I could almost see him asking where the hell his vocal censor had got to. Stammers have no loyalty. I made no move to answer, thinking that maybe to him it was a natural question. Maybe to his generation there was nothing to keep hidden, nothing essentially private and personal about B-linking. He'd grown up with it, had been plugging into the sims ever since he could see and feel on his own account. It wasn't something that had stolen into his life like some kind of succubus or social disease. And he wasn't what you might call socially sensitive.

What can you expect from a novice feeler?

But to me—and I don't deny that I'm way behind the times— B-linking was still a vice. It was still something that happened behind closed doors. So far as I was concerned, there was still virtue in not doing it.

Because he looked confused, and slightly bewildered by the way I'd clammed up, I finally said, "I don't use the link."

"Not for fights?"

"Not for anything."

He suddenly looked away. Perhaps he was angry. After all, the B-link was his career. It was his reason for living. And I'd just dissociated myself from his way of life as if it was something dirty. I wondered how to repair what I'd said.

Then, unexpectedly, he laughed. For once in his life he'd discovered a crazy thought. He laughed.

Then he said, "It's a—*good* thing there aren't more of you or I'd be—*out* a job."

"So you would," I muttered, looking over his head at a wasp circling someone else's face. The threatened individual was maintaining a sturdy dignity, but a girl with silver eyelids sitting next to him was tensing her jaw and praying hard the insect wouldn't drift her way.

Nobody dared swat the thing. They didn't want to get involved.

"But hell," he said, persisting in spite of it all, because he wanted to get it straight in his head, "fights are *real*."

"So's the murder rate in the suburbs," I retorted, irrelevantly.

We braked hard, long before the station, and everyone leaned into the deceleration patiently, as if we were all part of a well-rehearsed dance routine. It almost gives you a sense of belonging to know that inertia takes you all the same way at the same time. No one can buy immunity. That's equality for you.

In the station there was a flurry of violent action as those barging their way out squeezed through the gaps between those barging their way in. It was like a clumsy riffle-shuffle where the cards get redistributed fairly comprehensively but suffer agonies in the process. The overall situation didn't change, and though my wrist was aching I didn't bother to try for a seat.

After the nauseating process of getting under way again was over, I dragged up enough breath to say something else.

"Anyway," I said, "it's *not* real."

He didn't get the point. How could he?

"Well," he said, "the—*fight*'s a sim. But the *link*'s real. It's not a—*feeler*. It's live." Then he realized again that he was spilling out the obvious, and went red.

I shrugged, finally getting rid of the whole sorry question with a meaningless gesture. Sure, the charge that came over the E-link was straight from source. When you hooked into Herrera it was pure Herrera that resonated inside your brain. It was his pleasure, his desperation, his glory. Not a feeler hired to identify with the situation but a real live broadcast of real live emotion. The ultimate triumph of MiMaC. The big kick—what the vampires really lusted for. Real? Well, okay, it was real—

that way. But it wasn't any the less a Network product than Jimmy's beer commercial. It was a thin, carefully dissected slice of reality. A slice that was saleable. And it was processed and packaged just like anything else Network invested in.

I didn't want to talk about the fight. I didn't want to hear about it. I didn't even want to watch it, but there'd be no way I could keep myself away. A snake maybe feels the same way about snake-charmers.

I searched for something to say to sidetrack the conversation, but I couldn't find a thing. A blank mind. Jimmy Schell was so remote, in that moment, that he might have been one of those goddam knights-in-armor I'd been puppeting around for days—something that once existed but was no longer comprehensible, a figure carved out of matter but with no relativity. Like the girl in his commercial—a visual cue, a fiction of the holovisual image, pure simulation.

But he turned the conversation on his own, perhaps in search of a topic where we could establish some kind of *rapport*. He needed to feel comfortable. He was sensitive to mood and he knew he'd put me in a bad one. He wanted to soothe it over. That, I guess, is what Network calls *talent*.

"You lived in the stack for long?" he asked.

"Nearly twenty years," I told him.

"You must've had a—lot of neighbors."

"They come and they go."

Caps are like cells in a honeycomb. For solitaries. Most people don't stay solitary for long—not in a world where we all practice neurotic togetherness. People come to caps before, after and in between marriages. There are probably only ten or fifteen long-termers in a stack which houses six or eight hundred. I knew one or two in mine, but they were six or eight floors down, and we had nothing in common except staying power. The temps suited me—I had no use for anything enduring and permanent in the way of friendships.

"—*Maybe* you don't generally make—*friends*," he said—a weird sentence that could be anything from an indictment to an apology. The fact that he didn't know what he was getting at himself was signaled by the double hitch.

I just shrugged.

The train came in to our station, braking hard all the way. We joined in the squirming contest. I got out easily, but he got stuck. That's one of the penalties of being short and wide. Human bodies ought to be built for maneuverability in crowds. Evolution has no foresight. I waited for him, and then we flashed our cards and took the elevator down to the Street together.

Down below it was dim and dingy, though the sky was still dull gray and brown. Twilight comes early at ground level and lingers a hell of a long time. The real day only lasts as long as it takes the noonday sun to cross the gap between the highest ledges. We live in cliff faces, canyons and caves, men of the third Stone Age. But twilight lasts a long time, and we reckon we have durability.

"How long have you worked at—*Net*work?" he wanted to know.

"The same twenty years," I told him, exaggerating slightly. "Or damn near. Spares and stunts. Master of a million puppets." Old troupers never die—they just fade out to violins. I let myself go on, to pass the time while we walked. Time was slower now and the world was hard and steady again. "If I had a five for every sim I'd driven to its death I'd be in Consie City," I said, ruminatively. "I guess that's my forte—dying. Going out with a splash and a rattle. You think it's the hero and his fancy shooting gives the vamps that flash of satisfaction when the villain buys it, but it isn't. It's me. The feeler's inside the hero's head, but it's watching me go out that fires his little burst of glory. It's not just the winning—it's the way that he wins.

"I go down screaming, like it's a pleasure to kill me. We all need someone to look down on, someone to kick in the balls, someone to kill. That's where the real kicks come from, so far as the vamps are concerned. That's why it means something to them. They're getting their own back on the cruel world, on the crowds that hustle them every moment of their lives. It's the loser who gets the winner his big payoff. Life is a zero-sum game. Without me to go out like an exploding bogeyman there'd be nothing. You remember that when you're feeding a billion vamps what they love. Remember the poor sod who's handling your patsy."

I shut up then, feeling just a little bit cruel, although he'd never realize it or know why. He wasn't allowed to think like that, to be sarcastic about the sacred vocation. His mind had to remain pure. A feeler has to identify with the hero-situation all the way down the line. To him, the villain has to be so much filth to be swept up. He wasn't supposed to be thinking about the guy handling the sim—he was supposed to believe in it as if it were all real, whether it was the super space patrol or knights in shiny armor.

But he didn't mind me running off at the mouth. It was all the same to him. Just noise. Just something to talk at now his teddy bear was retired.

"You don't—*like* it much, do you?" he said, experiencing a flash of real insight.

"It's a living," I said. "And it's something I do damn well. I don't expect much else. It's an average kind of life. Never mind the quality, feel the width."

And it was enough. There had been a time—but isn't there always?

The dispensers in the lobby were half-full and working, which demonstrated that the supply company with the contract for the building was at least keeping pace with the local kids, whose mission in life was to get everything for nothing and bugger up the machines in the process. We both got supper packs, hanging around looking hungry while the microwaves got to work. I nodded at the building superintendent, who looked vaguely like a sheriff out of an antique movie. Then we took the elevator to the thirty-ninth, suspending the chat as we went. Nobody talks in elevators, even when they aren't packed tight.

We exchanged dutiful smiles as we turned to haul out keys for our separate doors. We each muttered something inaudible.

Once inside, relaxing like a deflated balloon, I pulled the foil off the supper pack. I accidentally ran the edge along my little finger and slit it from the nail to the first joint. I started to curse, and just for a second the syllable stuck in my teeth. I didn't know whether to laugh or try again until I got it right.

CHAPTER TWO

With the magnification turned up full the image filled the cap from the back wall to the central deck. I let the bed down and perched on it, with my legs folded under so I didn't have to dangle my toes in the fringe of the image.

The window was behind me and the million multicolored eyes of the neighboring capstacks were staring at the back of my head. I didn't bother with the screen. Sometimes, in between programs or when the chat got too banal to bear, I liked to turn over, make the bed into a bridge between the holo's fantasy world and the all-too-real city. I liked to look down both ways—into the consumer dream, into the night-ridden street.

I wasn't ever afraid of the height.

Living on the thirty-ninth floor for the best part of twenty years, in a capsule like a wormhole with one side all glass, is enough to cure anyone of acrophobia—or drive them mad. But I never had it. I liked the height. I guess I'm an acrophile, with no inborn fear of falling. I liked to be high up above the filthy street in 3912 Capstack 232, with the illusion of floating amid the towers of light, suspended in some kind of limbo, in the middle of it all and yet quite apart. Alone.

But for now, it was back to the world and eyes diving into the holo. The viewpoint was hovering over the ringside, looking down and across a neutral corner. The sim that Paul Herrera was running was, as usual, dark-skinned with silver trunks. The challenger, Angeli, wore the white skin and the royal blue gear.

Except for color, the two sims were identical. There was very little of the Negro about the features of the black body—they were the same neutral blend of racial characters as those of the white. The skin color differed only so you could tell the boxers apart with the utmost ease. Pound for pound, inch for inch, the bodies were matched dead equal. The fight was fair—as fair as computer programming and human ingenuity could make it. Even the rules were programmed into the simulation-pattern. Herrera and Angeli could make the sims do just about anything, so long as it was in the rules. If either of them tried to throw a foul punch or hang on when the break was called they would tie themselves in knots. It paid to stay legitimate—trying to make a sim do what it wasn't programmed to do threw your mind into confusion, and you left yourself open to get hurt. In sim boxing, all fights go by the book.

And the best man always wins.

The best handler, that is.

The bodies in the ring were just patterns of light, but to me and many millions of others they looked real. What's anybody but a pattern of light on your retina? They looked real, and they behaved as if they were real. To the men handling them they even felt real. They hurt when they were hit. They bruised and they cut, and their nonexistent bones could be broken. Everything was for real, until it was all over—and then Herrera and Angeli could step right out of their battered, agonized, maltreated bodies right back into their own sweet selves. No scars—except mental ones, which don't show. Sim boxers feel the pain, but they aren't supposed to get damaged. That's the theory. As to what goes on inside people's heads—well, that's not Network's business and it isn't in the retail-indexed package, except for emotional resonance.

In the days when men used to take their flesh with them into the ring it might be the strongest man that won, or the fastest, or the one with the longest reach, or the one who didn't cut as easily as the next man. But in the sim, all men were guaranteed equal, and the only difference was how well you could use what the machine had given you. A spastic dwarf and a walking mountain could hook up together and fight level. The man who won might be the cleverer, or the more skillful, but most likely he was the man who most desperately *wanted* to win, who could extract from the sim everything which it was programmed to give, and add the indefinable something extra that sorts out the winners from the losers.

And that man was Paul Herrera. Every time, for as many years as anyone could remember. Except maybe me.

Herrera had been a winner now for eighteen years. It would have been unthinkable, fifty years ago, for a boxer to last so long. Herrera had grown old as champion—but that didn't matter because he kept the same body with the same abilities. Eternal youth—physically, at least. As long as his mind didn't begin to crack or fade, as long as his spirit didn't fail, there could be another eighteen years in Herrera yet. He could keep on getting better, wiser, more skillful. And any novice coming into the game with youthful enthusiasm and high hopes had eighteen years to catch up.

There'd been a time, long ago. when Herrera had had nothing but the will to win. He'd won fights, but without much style, without much real ability in handling the sim. He'd lost a fight, too. But now he had it all. All the skill, all the experience. Year by year, it became more difficult to see anyone being able to take him. Other men who'd been in the game almost as long as he had were maybe just as clever, just as good, but they always had one thing they could never overcome—a psychological handicap. Some time back in their past, Herrera had beaten each and every one of them. They knew it, and he knew it. He was the king.

Everyone looking in, as I was, whether they were using E-link or had the commentary switched on or were just watching, knew that Herrera had to win tonight. No up-and-coming youngster like Ray Angeli, for all his vamp-appeal, could possibly take him.

But Angeli did have vamp-appeal. There could be no doubt about that. While the chat went on and Network's producers carefully spun out the anticipation, the meter in the corner of the sim showed that nearly thirty percent of the vamps were hooked into the challenger. Thirty percent is a lot of support for a loser. A lot of the thirty would be hitch-hikers, intending to drink what they could out of the kid and then jack him in—get out and leave Herrera to finish him, but there would be some who'd stay with him on the forlorn hope. By the time the writing was on the wall, though, he'd be down to five percent or less—freaks who charged up on negative E and oddballs who hated Herrera so much they'd cling on till the bitter end in the hope of seeing a lightning bolt from heaven split him in two.

I wondered, absently, as the fighters came to the center of the ring which of them Jimmy Schell would be riding. He'd asked me but he hadn't told me. My guess was Angeli. Angeli had the right qualifications to attract a kid like Jimmy. Jimmy could identify with Angeli's hopes—maybe tie them in with his own. But Jimmy wouldn't stay—not for long. He'd have to get out. He'd maybe even switch over to vamp Herrera for the K.O.—a shallow mind like his wouldn't feel uncomfortable about that. After all, he'd think, it's only entertainment....

The bell went and Herrera danced away, catlike, and Angeli came forward with too much eagerness, too much hurry. Angeli over-reached, got tapped, clinched, and then came away. He steadied himself, began to jockey for position, threw a couple of poor punches he didn't really mean, and got jabbed again for his pains. Herrera came in to hustle him a bit, and got in another short-range blow when the challenger tried to clinch. They tested each other's gloves, measuring one another's eyes as they settled into the rhythm of the fight. Herrera was taking it easy, coasting, waiting for Angeli to come to him.

The viewpoint swung so we could look first into the champion's face, then full at the challenger. Already, the difference was showing clear. The identical faces were worked into very different aspects by the minds that were wearing them. Angeli was handsome. Herrera wasn't. Angeli looked grim. Herrera looked vicious.

They danced, they faced up, waiting for the bell. Angeli threw a couple of punches at Herrera's head, but they were brushed aside by the dark sim's gloves. But this time Angeli was good enough to avoid the left hook aimed at his nipple. He was more careful now, more stylish, moving as if he meant it. There was no more clinching.

In the last few seconds of the round Herrera chased him, and couldn't catch him. In those seconds, Angeli looked good, like a man who could really handle a sim. He must have felt good, too, and his vamps would be getting their belt, sucking him up greedily. But the seventy riding Herrera must have been drowning in the feeling that it was all okay, that this kid was in the bag.

After the bell, neither fighter had really worked up a simulated sweat. The tally flashed the score, the round going to Herrera, but that didn't matter a lot.

At this stage of a fight, everyone is winning. Both fighters fancy themselves, are in to win. That's what the game is all about, from Network's point of view. First the contest, then the kill. It all pulls in the consumers.

In the second, the pattern of the fight began to develop clearly. There was a lot of movement as Herrera used the width of the ring to try and harass Angeli. Herrera moved faster and covered a lot more canvas. Angeli was more economical with his movements, more graceful. He refused to be reached and he didn't let Herrera steal space. The champion jabbed a lot, landing most of the punches but making no real impact. If only Angeli had been able to beat his opponent's guard he could have done some good, but style is ninety percent show—Angeli's brand of style, at any rate.

A couple of times Herrera seemed to be over-reaching, and Angeli went in with long looping rights, but Herrera ran round the blows with almost contemptuous ease. He was barely touched.

At this stage, both fighters were waiting—looking interested but scoring very little. Against a man of Herrera's proven stamina that seemed like a dangerous way for the challenger to play, especially with Herrera taking points in the early minutes that would have to be won back the hard way. But Angeli wasn't wearing himself out. He was looking easy.

In the third, though—with the second having obviously gone to Herrera—Angeli began looking to put in a greater quantity of punches rather than sparing himself to put one in that could hurt. For awhile, they looked to trade blow for blow, and for the first time Angeli's class began to show. He landed a couple of rights, cutting through Herrera largely by aggression, although he got solid raps in exchange. Herrera was content to go backwards instead of sideways for awhile, though his left was always licking round Angeli's face. In the last half-minute, Herrera was forced into defense while Angeli tested him, but he made no attempt to clinch and slow down. The round went to the challenger by a shade.

The meter showing the B-link balance was as steady as a rock. The vamps were cruising, the excitement carrying them along just nicely. Whichever boxer they were hooked into they were getting their money's worth, for now. It was all good clean fun. So far.

I was out of it, and glad to be. I even had the commentaries switched off, so that only the sim sound effects were coming through. I was watching the fight, not pretending to live it. I was detached, uninvolved, rational. Clarity of mind is a valuable thing, and I rate it too valuable to risk inside an B-link headdress. The kind of willful damage you can inflict upon your state of mind with drink or cigarettes or psychotropics is something to be very careful of. I saw no pleasure in strategic self-distortion. I tried to keep my interest in the fight an *objective* one, and tried to concentrate on the *art* of boxing rather than the guts.

Maybe, I thought, as I tried to fill the empty moments between rounds, my attitude toward height and my distaste for the B-link are related. I felt, somehow, as if I were *above* the vamps, on a loftier plane—spectating while they clustered round to drink the emotional substance from the orgy of conflict which they had created out of what was once, perhaps, a sport.

Perhaps, I guess, was the operative word.

Angeli took the fourth, again by a shade, and looked pretty good doing it. But we were by no means back to square one. Angeli knew now what he had only half-known before—that Herrera wasn't slowing down, wasn't easing up, wasn't impressed. Angeli was beginning to feel that the sim he was riding needed pushing along, dragging about the ring. The hammered flesh was beginning to weigh on him a little. But not on Herrera. The champ was still making the pace even if Angeli was edging the punches. If the challenger was going to do something real he was going to have to pull out more and keep pulling it out. Herrera still had reserves untapped, and always seemed to have. No one knew how much more Angeli might pull out—he had never been extended to his limit.

The fifth was dead even and even the computer declined to give a decision. The tally counter split the round two ways. Any difference there was in that round was between the minds of the fighters—the way they were taking their punches psychologically. Herrera, I knew, would be soaking it up, just feeding it back to his own gathering fury. Every time you hurt Herrera you made him that little bit better. I couldn't believe that the same was true of Angeli.

In a sense, Herrera was almost a vamp himself. He fed on emotion like his devoted fans. Where he got it from doesn't matter—it all welled up inside him, whether he sucked it from the air or his opponents or even his audience. Somewhere in Herrera there was a powerhouse where need was created, in defiance of the law of conservation of energy. They claim that the only kind of telepathy that exists is the bastard kind that exists courtesy of MiMaC, but any really top class performer, of whatever kind, will doubt that. When you're winning, you can prey on your victim's mind. You can absorb the flood-tide of feeling that's somehow always there. Herrera was sucking up Angeli and feeding on him, somehow. He knew he was winning, believed in himself, and he didn't need the machines to make his mind resonate.

Herrera took the sixth, and for a moment or two as the bell went and the gloves dropped the sim showed Angeli's face, and found within the eyes just a hint of defeat. Angeli felt he was pulling out the last of his stops, and the champ wasn't giving. Not an inch.

I could understand something of the doubt that was creeping into Angeli's soul. The vamps would be too high on his feelings to know or care about what he was thinking—and in any case that's something MiMaC can't do, because thoughts are transient, tentative, evanescent, and can't be captured. But I knew, because I'd been there.

What Angeli was thinking was this:

Herrera is moving faster and further than I am. He's burning up more energy. But he's not tiring. He's hitting just as hard. He doesn't get hurt. What do I have to do? What has to be done to break through? When and how does that facade ever waver, ever begin to fail.

And Angeli had one thought to fight against.

Eighteen years.

Like everyone else, Angeli knew there had to be a way to crack Herrera. That was a matter of faith, and a logical certainty. Paul Herrera was human, and had human limits. But where were they? And how did you have to go about pushing him beyond them. Angeli was thinking hard, and finding no answers. He'd find a hundred, in time—after the fight—and he'd be able to write off his defeat and carry on. But for now, he was going under. Slowly.

That eighteen years was one hell of a powerful testament to Herrera's invincibility. It was one hell of a fact to have rebounding in your mind—a thought to destroy your composure, to undermine your confidence.

Ray Angeli had been six years old when Herrera first took the title. He was too young to remember, but he was old enough to know. He knew that Herrera had started winning and never stopped, and that once upon a time he had hurt a man so badly that he had died of shame. That's hard knowledge to carry around, especially when you come to it so long after it's happened and become meaningful. It did no good at all for Herrera's opponents to know that he fought so hard that he had killed a man—not with punches but with sheer humiliation. Herrera was a man who could do damage—psychological damage—to his opponents.

Angeli wasn't scared. But he *knew*. And that has to make a difference.

It wasn't Herrera's fault, of course. It never had been. He only did what he was supposed to do. He just gave the mind-riders their big kicks. He was a feeler in a million. Maybe he loved winning more than any other man alive. He loved carving people into pieces. He gloried in the way he hurt them. If the vamps are addicts, what does that make Herrera? I don't know, but it still wasn't his fault that a man had died after facing him in the ring.

In an earlier age, Paul Herrera would have been a misfit, a crazy man. With his own body he could never have found an outlet for the things inside his mind. But in this age he had become an idol and an institution. He was the champ. That's the way the cards fall. And that was the way Ray Angeli had to look at them spread out all over his mind.

When they came out for the seventh I expected to see Herrera begin to tee up his man for the hammer. But Angeli was still tough, and he didn't let go of his style. He hung on in, taking on the champion and preserving the margin narrowly.

Through the seventh and the eighth and the ninth the fight ran on, as if frozen into a fixed regime, with change in abeyance, content to wait in the wings. Herrera was better, but he wasn't so much better that he could swing things entirely his way. Punches were going both ways—good punches—and it had all the makings of a really tough fight, hard on both men. The sim skins were showing the signs of hurt. Angeli's white body was staining red, and one eye was looking bad, seeping blood.

But the black face was beginning to inflate as the flesh took punishment. Herrera looked uglier by the minute. But nothing dramatic happened in all three rounds. If Angeli couldn't reach Herrera, he was damned sure he wasn't letting Herrera get to him.

I knew it had to break some time. I knew there had to come some elusive moment in the dimension of time in which some tiny event, of little intrinsic significance, would finally tip the scales and send them swinging out of true. Once the balance was gone the whole structure of the fight would tumble. It would turn into a massacre.

But in the meantime, Angeli held his vamps. He shored up his own hopes. He stayed on the tightrope, and stayed, and stayed.

The tally counter showed Herrera still ahead at the end of the ninth. Not by much, but enough to hang on to if he wanted to go the distance and take the fight on points. But that seemed unlikely. It wasn't his style.

Angeli won the tenth—one might almost say a shade luckily, if one accepted that there was any such thing as luck in a sim fight. When the sim zeroed in to show the world his face as he turned for his corner at the end of it that shadow of doubt—the thin lattice of thought that had foreshadowed his eventual defeat—was gone.

I wasn't fooled. There was nothing happening to rekindle my faint hopes that Herrera was booked for a fall.

By this time, both fighters would be in top gear and coming to the end of their emotional resources. The cruising had gone on long enough, and from the vamps' point of view it was time to climax. They'd had their ride, now they wanted their crash. By now, Angeli would have stopped thinking. His mind would be frozen over, feeling still, but not doing much else. Thanks to the miracle of MiMaC, however, the resonance link would still be strong—sweetness pouring out of the strong like a hive of bees, into the minds of the weak.

As they came out for the eleventh, I found myself praying that something might yet happen—that the dispelled doubt might be the signal for a change in the wind. It wasn't reason or experience that was urging me, but desire. I still wanted to see Herrera beaten. I always had. Sometimes, you just can't help yourself flying in the face of what you know to be inevitable.

I cared. I knew I was going to be disappointed.

In a hypocritical moment, I could tell myself that I wanted Herrera to lose because I disapproved of what he did for the vamps. I could tell myself that I was disgusted by the way they fed on him. And maybe that was true. The thought of countless emotional voyeurs enjoying orgasms every time Herrera threw a K.O. punch was pretty sickening. But in slightly less self-congratulatory moments I had to admit that there was more to it than that. I bore Paul Herrera a grudge.

And in the beginning of the eleventh, I was charging up— not, like the vamps, on the fighters' emotion, but on my own. I was getting excited, getting involved. Curled up on the edge of the bed I was tensing my muscles in sympathy. I had my fists clenched and held rigid. I wasn't waving them or pushing them, just holding them. But if Angeli had landed a good punch I would be able to feel it in one of those fists. I would get the tingling in the nerves as he hit Herrera hard.

Only he didn't.

Under my breath, I was urging Angeli on.

But he was going to pieces.

Herrera, with a burst of sheer power, came through Angeli's guard like a knife and landed a superb combination—left to the temple, right just above the heart.

Angeli went reeling. His arms went wild, and a third punch, which only glanced off him, put him down. He came up at seven, backed on to the ropes, tried to shield himself and pull Herrera into a clinch. He didn't make it, and went down to one knee to take eight, still wanting to come back and mix it.

Back he came, but without all the things which had made him into a contender, kept him going for so long. He couldn't keep the champ out, couldn't put together his own punches.

The bell came, and Angeli went to his corner to be brought

back to life, but it was all over. The tally counter no longer mattered, and the link meter was swinging.

Angeli had held his thirty right to the bitter end, but they were gone now. No one believed in him any more, and most weren't going to take what Angeli was going to take when he went back to be slaughtered in the twelfth. They were running—flopping back into their chairs in a blind, black drunk, overcharged and ready to let themselves sink. Only the real gluttons would switch to Herrera so late.

When the twelfth began, Angeli was holding just six percent, and even that seemed high. Old ladies hoping for miracles and groovers who lapped up suffering as well as—or instead of—exultation.

While Herrera took him apart, knocking him down for a full count half a minute before the end, I trudged down from the sorry heights of forlorn hope. I didn't want to watch what was left—I wanted to think about something else, but you can't switch off your eyes and somehow I couldn't move towards the controls. I saw it all happen.

There was no real backlash. After it was over, I knew it had always been the same way. I didn't feel disturbed. I was calm. My unclenched fists were resting easy on the blanket. I just shrugged off the sad adrenalin draining through my bloodstream, and instructed myself not to care.

Herrera had won again. So what.

I finally switched off the holo. Herrera would stay with his sim awhile yet so that the vamps could gorge themselves on his triumph a little time longer. It would slide away from its peak very slowly, ebbing away gently rather than plunging down. The connoisseurs reckoned that a better charge than the best of erotic spasms. *Chacun à son goût.*

I went to sort through some cassettes, looking for something to take my mind away. Somehow, everything I looked at struck me as being insipid. I found it difficult to choose one.

Then I tested the cut on my little finger, to see if it still hurt.

CHAPTER THREE

The bell rang.

I was in mid-dream, and the frail images fled away into the dark recesses of my mind. I was slowly decanted into consciousness. I opened my eyes, and found that it was almost completely dark. Only the wan glow of the city lights filtered through the cracks on either side of the window screen.

For a moment I was suspended, groping for the ill-formed memory of the bell and wondering what had dragged me out of my dreams. Then the sound came again, this time rudely shattering my drowsiness.

I turned over. A tell-tale light was glowing mutely on the console. The luminous dials on my wrist-set, which was hanging from its buckle beside the bed, told me that it was three in the morning.

I thumbed the switch which would enable me to speak to the lobby.

"You got the wrong number," I said. I wondered briefly whether kids had managed to break in and were dancing a finger-jig on the bells, waking up the whole building. If so, the superintendent would half-kill them. He was a mean man.

"Hart," said a voice. It was a brittle voice, guttural. It dragged out my name in a funny kind of dilute drawl. It wasn't asking a question. It knew who I was. No wrong number.

"Who's that?" I asked, trying to match his harshness in my own tone.

"I want to talk to you."

"In the morning."

"Now." He sounded confident as well as determined. He had a right to be. Anyone who goes out in the streets at three a.m. just to talk to someone has enough of a reason to get listened to. Also an armored car. Capstack concom is not the sort of district where you take a peaceful stroll.

"Who the hell are you?" I wanted to know.

"Name's Curman."

I'd never heard of him. It didn't surprise me. There weren't any acquaintances of mine with the habit of waking people up at this time.

"Are you a cop? An agency man?"

"No."

"Is the superintendent there?"

A new voice came over the mike. "It's okay, thirty-nine twelve," it said. "I checked his ID. It's clean. I got his gun."

The superintendent knew his job. He was the kind that lets innocent cap dwellers sleep at nights. Except when people come calling. He'd held the job seven years and was still calling me by my cap number, but that was okay. I'd be no worse protected for being a number.

"Send him up," I said.

"Thanks." This—dryly—from Curman.

There was a click as the phone link was cut. I got out of bed and groped for a pair of trousers and a shirt. I unlocked the door and switched the light on. While I waited, I looked around for something to do with my hands. I couldn't find anything, so I just jammed them in my pockets and twisted the keys around my fingers. I had an apprehensive feeling in my stomach. I still couldn't think of a reason why I should be gotten out of bed at this time. My instinct still said *cop,* though he'd denied it, but I had a crystal clear conscience for the month. Where law, order and security were concerned I was a real good joe.

There was a knock on the door, and he came in without waiting for his invitation to be renewed.

He was a tall man, looking thin because he was elongated

but not really lightly built. He had a dark face with a lot of fake worry lines. He also had bad teeth. I got the impression he had put a lot of practice into looking tough.

"You're Ryan Hart," he said. It still wasn't a question.

"What do you want?" I asked. It seemed like about the fifth time of asking.

It was his move, but he wasn't in a hurry to make it. He closed the door gently behind him, and looked around.

"Don't know how people live in these things," he said. He extended his long arms to touch both walls simultaneously.

"It's very fashionable," I said. "Not to mention public-spirited. We got a space problem in the city. People have to adapt their lifestyles. I'm in the vanguard of a great social movement. That's what the commercial said, anyhow. What do you want?"

"I live out of town," he muttered, uncommunicatively. He moved toward me. I didn't retreat.

"Got a drink?" he said—not aggressively. Almost ruminatively.

"Got a reason why I should give you one?"

"Sure," he drawled. "Makes it all feel better. Cuts the ice. You know. Eases the tension."

I slid out the locker and touched a bottle, looking at him. He shrugged slightly, and nodded. I pressed a glass to the catch and then passed it to him. It wasn't a double and I didn't bother asking him whether he wanted anything in it.

He stood there with it in his hand.

"You?" he asked.

"Too early," I said, sarcastically.

He shrugged. "I saw your program tonight," he said. "That was some ape."

I had to think hard to realize what he was talking about. I didn't know what the crud channels had been putting out that I might have done some fancy handling for. I didn't remember any apes. Not recently.

"So?" I said.

"We knew it was you," he said. "When the old man was

tracing you, they told him. I would've come earlier, only we sat through it. I don't know why."

He drained the glass in one gulp.

I stood and waited. I didn't want to waste any more breath.

"D'you see the fight?" he asked. Suddenly, there was a new note in his voice. He was getting to the point. I guessed then why he'd taken so long. He was weighing me up, studying me. There was something about me he couldn't figure. It was mutual.

"Yes," I said.

"Too bad," he commented. "About Ray. In with a chance until those last minutes. So far, then up in smoke. Pity."

"I cried myself to sleep," I told him, laying on the sarcasm hard because it didn't seem to be getting through.

He put the glass down on the ledge of the heater.

"You fought Herrera yourself once," he said. Again, it wasn't a question.

By now, I was ahead of him. I knew who he was and why he'd come. It was a shock. It took some getting used to.

"It was a long time ago," I said, flatly. "Before he was a champ."

Curman nodded, slowly. "You beat him."

"That's right," I said. "I beat him. A long, long time ago."

"You better get dressed," he said. "Properly. You have to come with me."

"Like hell," I said, not meaning it. Now it was me who wanted time to weigh things up, to try and understand. There was a chasm opening up before me. My life was being ripped in two. Now—many, many years too late. If it's ever too late.

"Velasco Valerian wants to see you," he said, gently.

I studied his face for thirty seconds or so. He wouldn't blink. Then I picked his glass up and put it in the sterilizer.

"You know," I said, letting my mouth run away with my thoughts, "sixteen or seventeen years ago I used to live most of my days expecting that someone might come to that door to tell me that Velasco Valerian wanted to see me. To me, then, it seemed like a thing that had to happen—that ought to happen.

A thing with some sense in it. I wanted Valerian to come to me, and I thought he'd have to. But time just went by, and nothing changed in the world. Valerian grew old, and I grew older. And nothing changed. The same ritual repeated itself over and over again. Tonight, it came to an end for—what is it now? Twenty-five? Thirty? And now me. But why? Why, after all these years? It makes no sense. Not any more."

I shouldn't have said all that out loud. It spilled out. Maybe I should have saved it all for Valerian. Maybe I should have bottled it up forever. But at three a.m. anyone can get caught on the hop. For a moment or two I was tilted by circumstance, and it all spilled. But it helped to clear my head.

Maybe I'd given it up, but it was here.

A chance.

What did it matter whether two years had gone by, or twenty, or two hundred? The long wait had been just that. In transit between phases of a life. Like a thirty-mile cruise on the mono-rail, frozen in a seat and whirled through a liquid world.

To arrive—where? By now, maybe it was a joke. A farce.

But I knew that Valerian played all his games hard, and this one hardest of all. He had to be up against the wall now, to have changed his mind after so long. I'd been squeezed out, but now I was in again. He had to be getting desperate. It wasn't a joke. Not so far as Valerian was concerned.

Suddenly, I felt a distinct and cold aversion to the idea of being a pawn in a sick drama. I revolted.

"Get dressed," said Curman.

"Go pick up your gun," I said, calmly. "I'll join you in the lobby."

"Pack a bag," he advised.

"Not yet," I told him. "I want to see Valerian first. Maybe after that I'll come back and pack a bag. But let's not take things for granted."

He shrugged. He was obviously a man who always took things for granted—a man so much at peace with the world and all it contained that he could *afford* to take everything for granted. It is given to certain people that they should find them-selves at home in their lives. He was probably a damn good bodyguard.

He left, shutting the door quietly. He moved softly, like a sneak-thief. I dropped my trousers and began getting into my underpants.

I took my time, and even buckled on my wrist-set with calm, deliberate precision. I could feel things swelling inside me. A little resentment, perhaps a little disgust for Valerian. Mostly, it was something indefinable—something heavy and warm.

Damn near twenty years, I thought, puppet-jerking spares. And now—I can jerk myself. As Valerian's puppet.

Like hell, I added.

I locked the door and went slowly along the corridor. I hadn't bothered to pack. Not even a gun. Curman would look after my health and safety.

The elevator, dropping thirty-nine floors, took a little of the weight off my stomach.

He was waiting for me, wearing a smile like a cheap plastic sphinx. He had a big black limousine down in the drop, looking very lonely. Nobody in the capstack had the credit or the pull to rate a car in these economically stagnant days. This car was a rude gesture directed at the world—all the things a car shouldn't be according to today's priorities. Such gestures are the prerog-atives of pure wealth—the toys of a rich man who doesn't have to bother courting public goodwill. Apolitical wealth, if there is such a thing.

The superintendent let us out through the double doors, holding his shotgun in the crook of his elbow. Absently, I wondered when he ever found the time to sleep. He probably didn't.

The car drove smoothly and silently. The capstacks loomed around us like fiery needles even at this time of night. Curman threaded a way through the maze of streets back to the arterial highway, and then he turned outwards, away from the urban complex. Valerian, I knew, lived a long way out—up in the foothills where darkness actually fell, and where the sun shone throughout the daylight hours. His home was his castle, and from its battlements he could look down at the sprawling city, the civilization which laid futile siege to his way of life. Valerian was determined to maintain feudalism as a living social system within his own little enclave, and he had the money to do it.

My eyes probed the shadows that littered the roadside, searching for the perennial population of gypsies and hitchers camping just beyond the city limits. But everything was quiet, nothing showed. Today's world doesn't shut down at night, but it watches from behind half-closed eyelids.

I didn't really want to talk to Curman, and he had said just about all he had to say to me. But he didn't like the silence, and he was easy enough in his mind to break it instead of putting up with it.

"Quiet night," he said.

"All the little mice are home in bed," I said. "Overloaded. Zapped out when their sets switched off. Network's contribution to bringing down the crime rate. More effective than the S.S."

"I thought it was the people who haven't got E-links who commit all the crimes," he said.

I didn't bother to respond to that. The exchange was pretty meaningless anyhow.

"You know Valerian well?" he asked.

"Never met him."

He glanced sideways at me then, his face showing his surprise.

"I thought—" he began, and then abandoned the sentence, not sure what he *had* thought. He tried again. "He talked as if he knew you. And you talk as if you knew him."

"Oh," I said, lazily, "we know one another. We just never met. We have this kind of mutual understanding. I think." I was willing to let it lie there. He had been content to let me wonder what the hell was what when he first rang my doorbell. Now I was willing to let him stay puzzled for awhile.

I inspected his profile from the corners of my eyes. His face had tightened slightly. Maybe he wanted to ask questions but didn't like to drop his act. He had his image to think of.

He settled for silence. We were too close to home for him to get the whole story. Valerian would be waiting. He drew away from me slightly, maybe because I wasn't what he'd expected.

Valerian's palace was at the top of a long shallow rise, along a private road through a small wood. The gates were pretty but I was willing to bet a lot that the tasteful aspect of the layout discreetly concealed some very effective equipment for discouraging ramblers. Even in the dark I could see that the gardens were pure kitsch—but yesterday's kitsch always becomes today's vanity. This place was something entirely disconnected from the reality of contemporary life: an alternative dimension, with its own cocoon of space-time and sense of values.

The doors of the underground garage were oak outside and good clean steel inside. They shut with a quiet firmness.

"Don't make too much noise," said Curman, as we got out and shut the car doors. "Mr. Valerian appreciates discretion."

"He receives all his visitors this way?" I queried.

"Only when the mood takes him."

The mood, apparently, had taken him pretty suddenly. My guess was that it had taken him within minutes of Ray Angeli getting knocked over, and had built up to some fairly monstrous proportions. I didn't expect to find Velasco Valerian at his best.

We went upstairs, into the dark corpse of the house. Curman turned on a couple of stair-lights so we could find our way, but it was all very discreet. In the capstacks, light is harsh and glaring, stripping all situations naked. But here it was muted. Valerian probably liked to live inside a cloak of shadows.

He was waiting for me in his library. It was a beautiful room with bookshelves instead of walls and big bookcases forming a cross in the middle. Eight or ten thousand books, all old—the legacy of a century of more-or-less mindless acquisition on the part of Valerian's immediate forefathers, carefully constructing an image. They could never have read the books—not even a tiny fraction—but that wasn't important. Like the black car, another of the obscene gestures of pure wealth: the acquisition of purposeless property and its non-functional display. Valerian was not the man to be embarrassed by the aura of such vanities. He probably felt at home here. Maybe he even took the books out now and again to finger the sad quality of the binding.

He was enveloped by a deep, high-backed chair, wine-dark in the light of a small lamp to the side and set slightly back. His face was mostly in shadow, but he must have been able to see me quite clearly as I stood before him.

"You're Ryan Hart," he said, smoothly, giving it the inflection of a polite question.

"Your handyman would have to be a fool if I wasn't," I replied. My voice was too sharp, the comment slightly ridiculous. My hostility was showing but not biting. I felt compelled, though, to make the gesture. Men like Valerian can't be defied, but you have to act as if they can. I hadn't come just to lie down and be counted.

"Sit down," he said. His voice was soft. He wasn't amused or annoyed or impatient—which meant that the fury which had overtaken him as Ray Angeli bit the dust was now perfectly controlled and disciplined.

I sat down, in a chair that was the twin to his own. There was a small table between us, where a book might be rested temporarily. There was no book. Valerian didn't go in for that brand of staginess.

"You sent for me?" I said, injecting a dishonest low-key anger into my voice.

"I have a proposition for you," he said. Unlike Curman he wasn't about to beat around the bush in order to see what came running out. Curman had stayed with us, but he was back in one corner of the room, looking at the titles on the spines of the books. He was listening very carefully.

"Go ahead," I said.

"I've followed your career," he said. "In a casual manner. I've retained an interest in your abilities. I think that you're wasted in your present work. You have talent above and beyond that required for simulation stunt work."

He paused, but I didn't bother to interrupt. I figured that it might as well all come tumbling out, hypocrisy as well. All as scripted. There was no need to slash at the curtain of soft lies. Not yet.

"You," he continued, "are one of the few people with a genuine mastery of the active component of mind/machine communication. I think you ought to be involved in it actively, ambitiously. I think you should go back into sport."

"Boxing?" I asked, ironically.

"Of course."

"No," I replied, flatly.

The refusal didn't shock or upset him. He didn't believe it. He leaned forward just a little, and the dim light caught his white eyebrows. There was sweat glistening on his forehead.

"No regrets?" he asked.

"Not your kind," I replied. That was a better one, but it didn't score. It failed to jerk anything out of him. He settled back into the shadow, to watch me without his own eyes being visible except as the faintest of gleams. His face was a blur.

"I want to back you," he said. "I should like to help you redeploy your talents more profitably."

"You want to make me a star?"

"A champion."

"You want me to beat Paul Herrera for you."

He made no reply to that, but was content to wait.

"You know I'm blacked," I said.

"And you know I have the power to set aside that ban," he said. "Circumstances have changed since that—unfortunate decision."

"How?" I said, almost spitting the word at him.

He wouldn't answer that, either. I changed the question to, "Why now?"

"Had you—" Here he paused suggestively, then went on, "—given up hope?"

"Hope!" Again I spat the word out as if it were poison. "Is that what you think? You think I've been wasting my life in hope—waiting for you to come to me and say, 'I've reconsidered. It's all forgotten and forgiven.' Do you think I've had no ambition in life but to serve your miserable purpose and knock all hell out of Paul Herrera? No, I haven't given up hope. Not that kind. I don't want to go back to the ring to fight your battles. The hell with your crazy vendetta."

"But you want to go back," he said, quietly. "To fight your own battles."

I waited a minute, letting myself calm down, not wanting to go off like that again.

"I used to." I said. "A long time ago."

"Not any more?" he said, challenging the implication.

"Not any more," I confirmed.

Valerian let a moment slide by. Then, abruptly, he told Curman to switch on the light. Curman didn't have to move far. He was waiting right by the switch. The electric chandelier flooded the room with yellow radiance, the four arms of the cross-shaped array of bookcases blooming forth with thin shadows while the gloom was dispelled.

I looked Valerian in the face, as he obviously intended that I should.

He was old. Not, perhaps, merely in years—he was maybe seventy, and could have had a long way to go if he hadn't lived those seventy so hard. He was old in terms of expended effort and hard driving. A charged-up metabolism and a diabolic energy had used and wasted him, had left him derelict. He had lived at an accelerated pace, consuming himself ravenously.

He looked at me now from a crumpled face like a screwed up piece of paper. His hair, his eyebrows, the thin beard, were all dirty white. His eyes were brown flecked with yellow and gray.

I realized why he had retired into shadows. The voice was the best of him that remained. It had kept its timbre, the quality and sureness that his features had lost.

"Do you see me?" he said, harshly.

I mustered my reserves of cruelty. "Should I care?" I said. "We all got troubles."

"My heart," he said, in a measured monotone, "has plastic valves and an electric motor. I plug in to my kidneys."

"You're a lucky man," I said. "Some people have to do without."

"I'm not asking for your sympathy," he said, "I'm demanding your understanding. You know what I want from you. You must know why I come to you now.

"You know—and you've always known—that I'd rather it was someone else, rather it was anyone except you. But now, after all this time, there can be no other way. Angeli was the last. No young man can beat Herrera, and no young man ever will—not until his mind begins to rot. I can't wait. Not any more. Another year will see me dead, and it has to see Herrera dead too. Literally, or metaphorically. He has to be beaten—and it needs a man who understands fighting, and who understands Herrera."

He might have gone on. But he'd already said more than enough. Perhaps more than he'd said in a good many years. We were even now—we'd both spilled out what we felt.

"That's it, is it?" I said. "I'm your last resort. You've been saving me up, locked away in a safe inside your memory. Now, when you figure you've reached your last crack, it's back to the beginning, back to Ryan Hart. Eighteen years of leading lambs like Ray Angeli to the slaughter, and then, just like *that—da capo.*"

"It has to be," he said.

"No," I told him.

"You have an alternative?"

"Sure," I said. "I have the alternative. The alternative is no. How the hell do you think I feel? I was a fighter once, and then I wasn't. I was blacked. Hounded out. In those days there was nothing I wanted more than to fight again. The fact that I was good—the fact that I was maybe even better than Herrera—

made it all the worse. I was a winner who couldn't even fight. And I wanted my chance back. I knew then that the only way I was likely to get back into the ring was with your backing. I *waited* for you. You needed me, I needed you. But where were you? For eighteen years, where were you? And you think that now you can lose your temper at three in the morning, and right out of the blue you can say, 'Where's Ryan Hart? Find him. Fetch him'.

"Do you think those eighteen years count for nothing? Do you think I'm the same man now that I was then? I know *you* are. But not me. Those eighteen years came out of my life, out of the good years. And I *counted* them—to me they mean something. It's too late, Mr. Valerian. It's sixteen, seventeen, eighteen years too late. There's no going back now."

"You have to," he said.

"An offer I can't refuse?"

"If you like. I can take your job, your home, your life. I can buy you. But it doesn't come down to that."

"You can threaten me all you want," I said, scratching my cheek. "But there's a nice banal saying. You can drive a horse to water but a pencil must be lead."

"I don't have to threaten you," he said. "Because even if you do hate me worse than you hate Paul Herrera, you want to get back to the ring. You want to win. And you'll do it whichever way you can." He said it with a curious note of triumph in his voice—the certainty of a man who knows that he is right and who knows that even if he is wrong he can enforce what he is saying. *I may not know what I am talking about but I will defend to the death my right to say it—and make it stick.* That's justice—the exclusive brand.

Velasco Valerian only had to reach out and take what he wanted. Right now, I was inside his fist.

Trapped.

And he was right. I would fight. I would win. I would do my utmost to avoid winning *his* way, and use every scrap of my ingenuity to get what I wanted without compromising, but I would win. I had to.

At long last, the moment had come.

I stared at him, and he knew that the understanding he had demanded was there.

CHAPTER FOUR

We rode the elevator up to the thirty-ninth just as the milling hordes were clamoring to ride it down. The working day was launched and on its way.

I wouldn't have been with them anyway—I had a couple of days off owing to me—but I couldn't help feeling alien as I jostled with them, heading in the wrong direction and not intending to turn back. Not ever.

As I walked along the corridor to 3912 Jimmy came out of 3909. We almost collided.

"—*Hey*, Mr. Hart," he said, in a tone far too jocular to be decent at eight-twenty, "you're going the wrong way."

I clapped him on the shoulder and made as if to go right on past him, saying, "I know it, kid, I know it."

He didn't get it. He was suddenly frozen, the wheels of his mind sticking as he tried to follow me with one eye and look Curman over with the other. Curman was behind me, carrying a big suitcase Valerian's valet had lent me.

"He looks like a gangster because he is one," I told Jimmy. "I'm being snatched by a millionaire and held to ransom. My intellectual chastity is in deadly danger."

Not unnaturally, this didn't do a lot for the kid's state of confusion. He was going purple with the effort of getting his ideas under way again.

"Sorry, Jimmy," I said, a little more gently, stopping to face him. "I won't be going in today. I won't be going in when I'm due back on Monday either. I quit. I'm going to work for Velasco

Valerian."

He looked a little disappointed. Things had moved too fast and left him stranded. He'd figured me for a human contact, something to hang on to in a world which was still, from his point of view, fearful in its pace of change. I had been his first barricade against the amorphousness and indifference of life in capland. Now I was gone. Like that. That's the way it is, of course. There's nothing you can depend on for long. But in this particular instance, he was unlucky. He'd come in at exactly the wrong moment.

"I'll be dealing with Network," I told him. "Though not quite in the same way. We'll maybe run into one another at the studios. You'll hear about me, and I guess I'll hear about you. Look me up and say hello. Okay?"

He was still just staring at me, with bewildered eyes. He couldn't string any words together—no words that he could get past his block. He just nodded, and then he went on his way, uncomprehending.

I looked after him, finding the thought that he cared faintly ironic, faintly—though I don't know why—disturbing.

I opened the door to the box that had been my home for as long as I could call anywhere a home. I went in, and wasted no time unsealing all the folding units where I had things stacked and stored. Opened up like that, the capsule was like a flower in bloom. Everything all over the place, with no space left.

Curman threw the case open and stood back by the door.

"Want any help?" he asked.

I told him I didn't. It was my life I was uprooting and ripping apart.

He watched me sorting through things, shoving the shards of my personal history into the case. His attitude toward me had changed completely since he'd watched me sparring verbally with Valerian. Last night he'd picked me up like a package, but now he didn't know what the package contained. He was uneasy with me. He felt like an outsider because he didn't know what was going on between his boss and me. It dated from before his time.

He hadn't said anything while he drove me back, but his hands and mind had been partially occupied then. Now, standing in the doorway watching me, he had nothing to do with himself but think. Curiosity kills cats, and they have nine lives, but most humans still haven't the sense to steer clear of it.

"You never met Valerian before last night?" he began, tentatively.

"I never did," I said. "But we didn't need any introductions."

"Not many people talk to him that way."

"I do," I said. I carried on carving up the stuff in the lockers and the folding drawers. There wasn't very much I wanted to take, but I was afraid that there was something I'd regret having left at some time in the unknowable future. I kept hesitating over decisions.

"What've you got against him?" he asked.

"He could have had me back in the ring eighteen years ago. He didn't. Also, I don't like him."

"What's he got against you?"

"He doesn't like me either."

"Ah, shit," he said, losing his cool just a little. "Are you going to tell me or aren't you?"

I thought of saying *no*, but then I thought *why the hell not?*

"It's a long story," I said. "At least, it is the way I tell it. And it hasn't much of a punch line."

He shrugged.

I sighed. I took two bottles out of the cupboard and gave them to him. I got a couple of glasses, and held them out. "We might as well get rid of the stuff," I said.

He poured.

"It's still too early," I said, inspecting the stuff, "but we may as well celebrate my immense good fortune. It's not every day your lifelong ambition comes true."

I sat down on the bed. He leaned against the wall, and eased the door shut behind him.

"Beginning of story," I said. "I was a boxer once. In my

formative days. I beat Herrera—they were his formative days, too. We were both young, both inexperienced, both learning slowly. Paul, I guess, was learning a little more slowly. Nobody else beat him, so I'm the only one. But that's just how things fell out. It could have been someone else."

He was nodding. He already knew all that.

"In those days," I said, "MiMaC wasn't as big as it is now. It was in use, it was working. But they were still exploring ways to exploit it. Big money men like Velasco Valerian would hold conferences and they would ask one another how they were going to sell this new miracle of science to the world—how best they could employ it to multiply their already-considerable fortunes tenfold.

"Everybody knew it was the biggest thing since the opposable thumb, and so everyone was very careful. People were anxious about it—about the way it could and might be used. Different interests were anxious for different reasons.

"Network was putting out E-link programs and B-link commercials, but the whole thing was in an experimental phase. Hardly anyone had actually bought the equipment—Network had to practically give headdresses away in order to explore the possibilities. Nobody knew enough about the marketability of the fake stuff—the new-style acting—that was being put across with the system. It had novelty value but no one could really be sure that it would ultimately become part of the structure of social life.

"They were slightly more sure of the marketability of the real thing—the live broadcast of the resonance effects of actual emotion. The one thing Network were reasonably sure of was that a whole new dimension could be added to televised sport—competition of all kinds. In a hard, tough game of any kind most men generate enough excitement to hype up an audience, even if they're only watching the damn thing. When they can actually hook in, identify with their hero all the way down to his emotions, the involvement is much greater and the hype that much better. And games have a recognizable form—the emotion is for a limited period and it builds up to a climax when someone wins and someone else loses. MiMaC provided limitless scope for the marketing of broadcast sport.

"But it wasn't quite as simple as that. Switching sport out of physical reality and into a holovisual sim made the process of mind/machine communication involved in handling the sim one with the process of broadcasting ER. But switching sport from the real world to a computer simulation was something which had to be sold to the people. It was an idea many people reacted against. Network stressed the fairness of the new sport and its genuineness as a competition of skill, but the real hook was the E-link—that was their banker bet, the key to the whole thing.

"Boxing, where one man faces one man and the climax of the contest is often a K.O. was just made for E-link broadcasting. And Paul Herrera was made for it too. He was—and is—good at handling a sim, but the chief thing which made him into a big Network asset was the fact that he was—and is—an extremely powerful broadcaster. The voltage in his brain during a fight is way above norm. He was a man with deep, rich, saleable feelings. He took—and still takes, after all these years—a savage delight in taking his opponents apart.

"Network took up Herrera and prepared to build a big market campaign on his ability to win and his capacity to glory in winning. He was their pride and joy, their ace in the hole. They needed Herrera—or, at least, they believed that they needed him.

"Of all the possible uses and applications of MiMaC, the one the men like Valerian—the men with money to invest—staked most upon was fight promotion. Maybe that's crazy, and an awful lot of people thought so at the time. Maybe it's just a commentary on human nature and the vagaries of the economic system—and one might add in that context that the government money which poured in to R & D concerned with MiMaC was overwhelmingly dedicated to the military applications. However—there was no shortage of eager fighters, men who'd always wanted to be fighters but were disqualified for physical reasons. Even a couple of real fighters, who were on the way down in the real-life game and saw a chance to apply their know-how in a new field, came to Network. Network financed the fighters, trained them and matched them.

"They had a monopoly, of course. They were the only ones with the machines, with the programs, the only ones who would put up the cash to present a bout. They had sole governance over the fighters, and they stage-managed the presentation of the game all the way from invention to world championship as if it were a gigantic advertising campaign. And, in a way, it was.

"It worked. It was a great success. A lot of things all happening together made E-link into a social institution, but boxing was probably one of the most important. The fight game—and Herrera—sold the biggest kick of all, and the kick sold E-link.

"It was necessary to Network that everything should go smoothly in their grand campaign. They couldn't afford any slip-ups. And there was just one slight hitch. For the most part, the most successful of their fighters were the men who radiated best. The winners were, for the most part, the guys who needed to win more than the rest, who got a bigger kick *themselves* out of winning. With all else equal, that's not really surprising. But it didn't apply all along the line. Some good broadcasters were lousy fighters. And one or two good fighters were very poor broadcasters.

"I was a good fighter. But across the B-link, I was rubbish. I fought coldly and methodically. I was skillful and clever, but not emotionally involved. I wanted to win—I always wanted to win—but somehow that wanting didn't translate itself into the kind of emotion that resonates through the machine-link. I don't feel in the way that Network wanted me to feel. And they couldn't afford to include me in their ambitions. I was a poor risk. Most of all, they couldn't afford to have me challenging for their world title. So they blacked me. They banned me from any participation in sim boxing. They did it less than a week after I beat Herrera and showed them what I might do. They got rid of me."

I paused to look at my captive audience, making sure he was still with me. He was, but from his point of view we hadn't got to the point yet. He still didn't see what it had to do with Valerian. He started to say so, but I didn't wait.

"It was a logical decision," I said, without bitterness. "They couldn't take the risk. Network had to put on a series of fights to really blow the minds of the vamps, create a spectacle whose kind had never been experienced before. The atmosphere of the gladiatorial arena multiplied a thousandfold—everything that sport had ever offered to its audiences, and more besides. So who needs a potential disaster? My only qualification for boxing was the fact that I was good. I could win. That wasn't Network's top priority. They weren't interested in that kind of best man winning.

"Velasco Valerian was in on the decision to have me blacked. With his pull, he could have reversed it, but he didn't. All for very good and practical reasons, you understand. It was that decision which meant that on the night Herrera won the title the wrong man was facing him in the ring. Instead of the best fighter it was the best feeler—a kid who might give the vamps orgasms but who was never, not in a million years, going to beat Paul Herrera. But what did that matter? Network were putting on a show. And, of course, it was obvious that no one could really get hurt. It could have been lions versus Christians if that had made a better spectacle. Only the sims took the punishment. Only the sims—and the minds that were running them.

"The kid that fought Herrera for the title died. Not because of what Herrera did, but because of the way he was made inside. And, of course, he died decorously enough, in the hospital, long after the switch was off. He'd done his job. The death wasn't blamed on Network—how could it be? It didn't even harm their big advertising job. It was played down that much. The fault was in the fighter, not in the system. So said the coroner. No one was to blame.

"But the kid that died was Velasco Valerian's son, and Velasco had his own ideas about blame and justice. He couldn't accept what the coroner said. He had to hold his own inquiry, inside his mind, and decide according to his own tenets just who was guilty. He started from two basic and inviolable premises: that no possible blame could be attached to his son, and that no possible blame could be attached to himself. That was fundamental to his whole approach.

"And the high court of Velasco Valerian's feudal vanity brought back two findings. One: that Paul Herrera was guilty of destroying his son, and two: that Ryan Hart also had to take a portion of the blame. The first was necessary in order to justify the first premise: it wasn't Franco that cracked up, but Herrera who cracked him. The second was necessary to justify the second premise: it wasn't Network's decision about priorities, which was partly Valerian's, that was responsible for Franco's being in the ring that night, but the fault of the man who should have been in his place. Velasco blames me for not being able to broadcast, for being the kind of man I am. He has to blame me, in order to avoid taking any of the blame himself.

"It's not as clear as that in his mind, of course. He probably hasn't worked it out. He doesn't know what he thinks—only what he feels. And what he feels is concentrated hatred for Herrera, diluted hatred for me. Unjust, maybe—but whenever did feelings respect justice?

"And that, basically, is it. All tied up with a pink ribbon. End of story. Except that near the end the plot sickens. Because Velasco discovers the thing that Ryan Hart knew all along—that the only way Valerian is going to engineer the ritual destruction of Paul Herrera is by matching him with Ryan Hart. A cruel twist of ironic fate, you may say. The innate comic justice of the way the world goes, maybe. Either way, a tangled knot. One that can't be untied, but only cut. End of story—all except for punch line. But I told you there was no punch line. Not yet. In time—"

I let it go.

The silence that fell was limp and haggard. It extended itself slowly, tiredly.

"You're crazy," said Curman, finally, pouring himself another drink.

"So's he," I replied. "Aren't we all?"

But of course, we aren't. Curman wasn't, for one. He was okay. He knew the way of the world. He cooperated, with the occasional shrug of his shoulders. He let things go on the way they were. He probably never wondered who was to blame for anything.

I resumed packing, leaving him to think. It probably didn't make any sense to him. There were probably a lot of things about other people's actions and motives that didn't make sense to him. But he always made perfect sense to himself. He had his wants and his needs clearly mapped out in the cosy little space that was his imagination. He led a disciplined life.

If everyone else were like him, the world would be a much easier place to live in.

"But why now?" he said, "after so many years."

"You were there," I said. "You heard him."

Curman had heard him, but Curman had been unable to comply with the demand for understanding. Curman *didn't* understand.

But I knew. For once in his life Velasco Valerian was having to compromise with the way that chance had stacked the deck. He was having to accept one of the decisions of fate. For him, it was the end of the road. Mortality had got him in the end. You can't fight the four horsemen. Everyone arrives at his own private apocalypse, someday.

CHAPTER FIVE

The first ordeal I had to face following my introduction into the Valerian household was breakfast. I didn't want any, but I didn't get the option. It was phase one in my adoption program. Valerian wasn't just hiring me, he was absorbing me into his particular form of life. I think the theory is called "indoctrination by example". Or something.

By the time Curman and I got back to the rotting mansion and dumped such of my erstwhile life as was portable it was late—nearly ten. Valerian, a creature of casehardened habit, had eaten at his usual hour. But he stayed to preside.

The meal, like the house and the fittings and the life Valerian had molded, came out of the past. I guess the aristocrats of finance have always taken advantage of their privilege in separating themselves and their whole personal environment from the turgid present and the ugly world they prey upon. All vultures are graceful flyers.

So breakfast was a time-machine, a doorway into a myth-world where everything was pretense and pretentiousness. There was an abundance of servants. I saw five. I didn't know what their official denominations might be, so I thought of them all as waiters. Good servants are so easy to find nowadays— that's the benefit of labor redeployment planning, the industrial army and the multiple redefinition of work.

The taste of the food meant nothing to me. It was too foreign. I'd been eating out of plastic packs all my life, and to me, that was real. Eating was a function, not a vice. In times of resource crisis, that's the way it has to be. But there were no crises inside Valerian's time machine. It was exempt.

I ate calmly, maintaining an attitude of careful self-assurance. Valerian watched me. Curman ate with me, as was obviously his habit. He was Valerian's good right hand, not just a hired gun.

The table had been originally set for four, and I tried to add that up. Valerian had eaten but the last place remained empty. I figured that if someone in the house was accustomed to eating at any old time instead of sticking to the timetable he or she had to be family. I couldn't quite work out what family Valerian might have. Franco had been his only child and the old man's wife had long since given way to the pressure and departed for a kinder existence, or lack of it.

The coffee was brought in, solemnly and with ceremony. I could hardly conceal my fascination for the way the minutiae of life were so carefully structured.

"Did you enjoy the meal?" asked Valerian, politely. I could see that he was ready for a sarcastic reply.

"How much did it cost?" I asked, quite blandly.

"Does it matter?"

"I don't know," I countered. "Does it?"

"In nutritional value, of course," he said, "the food you're used to is at an advantage. It gives you what you need without any other considerations being taken into account. But this food has aesthetic qualities which you may care to learn to appreciate."

"I don't think I need antique vices," I said. I didn't think I could learn them either. I'd been brought up with the idea—carefully nurtured by government propaganda—that food is fuel, that eating is a boring necessity with no more inherent pleasure than elimination or excretion. That's the attitude which has to be evolved to meet circumstances of supply-limitation. Valerian had lived since the moment of his birth with a different system of values. Neither of us could change, and it was futile for Valerian to be laying down that kind of challenge.

"Some people," I pointed out, quite inoffensively, "find self-indulgence rather obscene."

"You don't believe in obscenity," he said.

"No," I conceded, gracefully, "I don't suppose I do."

"I think you'll adjust to us, Mr. Hart," he said. I had no difficulty winkling the hidden meaning out of that one. That was the point he'd been trying to make. Was it worth it?

I realized something that hadn't been obvious in the gloom of early morning. Velasco Valerian was not a very clever man.

"I'll get along," I assured him. "I'm pretty tolerant."

He didn't say anything more. He'd declared himself and his aims. He was on to a loser. I wasn't going to change. I wasn't going to twist myself into something that would fit his script for a futile revenge. I was going to do it my way. There was to be no alliance, no compromise. He owed me eighteen years, and he was going to get nothing in return for what he was giving me now.

I suspected, though, that the fight against Valerian might be as hard as the fight against Herrera.

The door opened and a girl came in. She stopped dead in surprise—she obviously hadn't expected to find Valerian here, and with company to boot. Her eyes went first to him, and then to me. She almost changed her mind and went away again, but not quite. After momentary hesitation she came in and took her place at table. Like the genie out of Aladdin's lamp a waiter appeared. In a house like Valerian's the walls don't need ears. They're telepathic.

She ignored Curman as if he was part of the furniture. "Don't get up," she said. To me.

I hadn't. Her tone suggested she wasn't serious.

"Mr. Hart," said Valerian, "this is my granddaughter. Stella, this is Ryan Hart. He's a boxer."

She looked at me, her eyes saying something to the effect that I didn't look like a boxer. The name obviously meant nothing to her. I sensed a gulf between Valerian and his heir. I looked back at her. She had to be Franco's daughter. I hadn't known

Franco had a daughter. My mind did some quick arithmetic. She looked sixteen but was presumably older—unless Franco hadn't known he had a daughter either. She was slim and small, with straight hair and a face which hadn't yet grown to the potential of its features.

"Don't stare," she said, flatly.

I looked away, at Valerian. He didn't say anything but I thought he was mildly amused.

The waiter put a plateful of joy in front of Miss Valerian. She didn't look joyful. Another waiter whispered something in the old man's ear. How wonderfully, comically discreet, I thought.

"Excuse me," said Valerian. He went out.

I let my eyes stray back to the girl. She was staring at me. She obviously had no sense of justice. One-way protocol. I glanced at Curman, but he was in a world of his own, thinking peacefully. He didn't get involved in family affairs.

"You didn't waste much time," she said, conversationally.

"*I* didn't waste much time?"

She shrugged. "Either way," she said, "You're here." She didn't sound as if she resented it, but she didn't sound as if she approved. The continuing saga of grandfather's boxers and their quest for the unholy grail probably left her cold. She must have lived all her life in the midst of it and she was at the time of life when you get disenchanted with whatever you're in the middle of.

I tried to think of a question which retained some vestige of diplomacy, but couldn't. I began to hope that she'd help me out. She did, after her fashion.

"You're too old," she said.

"Just old enough," I told her.

"You're supposed to be the angel of death," she said. "You don't look the part. No way." Her tone was level, slightly mocking. I guessed she'd picked up her habits of speech in the wrong kind of company. She wasn't exactly a charmer.

"I'm just a fighter," I said. "Your grandfather's the one with angelic pretensions."

There was a brief pause while she chewed and swallowed. Obviously she didn't talk with her mouth full. There's something to be said for everybody if you look hard enough.

"I quite liked Ray," she said. "But I guess he won't be back. He'll have gone where all the failed angels go."

"Hell?" I suggested.

"The city," she replied. It wasn't original, but Curman smiled briefly, interrupting his silent contemplation of the infinite.

"I guess there's a regular cycle," I said. "A kind of system. The boys appear, go through the works, and then go. A complete processing—from hopeful to failure in seven stages. And poor you wakes up every ninety-ninth morning to find a new face at breakfast and another dream in ruins in the trashcan. The old wheel of fortune just keeps on rolling, and there's nothing new under the sun."

"Very poetic," she said, grinning faintly to herself. "Very boring."

I decided that diplomacy could go wherever the failed angels went.

"Do you care?" I asked. "Does the nobility of the quest to avenge your father help your little world go round?"

She liked that. I could tell.

"No," she said.

"But your granddaddy loves you anyway?"

"Fuck off," she said. I think I strayed over the limit.

She seemed to lose interest then, and devoted her attention to her food.

Curman nudged me, and stood up. "Let's go," he said.

I tried to catch her eye as we went out, to semaphore an apology with my eyebrows, but she wasn't allowing it to be caught. It didn't matter. I knew it wasn't goodbye, and there'd be plenty of time to heal the breach if it needed to be healed.

I went with Curman out behind the house into the grounds. About a hundred yards away from the house and its satellite buildings there was a small, squat edifice with no windows. This was where the action was.

It housed a holo unit with a twice-life-size image capacity, a number of E-link receiver sets and a couple of simcontrol units. Even Valerian didn't own a computer with the capacity to stage a fully-comprehensive situation-simulation, but he had a private hook-up to a machine which had—not one of Network's machines but one owned by an Industrial Research Corporation which used it for experimental purposes. Valerian probably owned more than half the company, and if research was slowed down because he requisitioned too much computer time, that was mainly his loss.

Waiting for us with Valerian was an assorted company. Apart from the technical staff there were two men and a woman. I was introduced to them one by one.

The first and least important was Ira Manuel, a fighter. I tagged him immediately—he was small and pale, with a grim look about his face, the kind of guy who, thanks to an accident of birth, got handed out a body which didn't fit his character, and who used the sim to try and correct nature's mistake.

The second man was Carl Wolff—a man I knew slightly from way back. He was a trainer. He was one of the handful of men who'd been recruited to sim sport from the old-style real version in the very beginning. He had a real interest in the new medium and he had a substantial contribution to make in helping adapt the knowledge and experience of the old game to the new circumstances. Most trainers are hard men who drive their fighters but Wolff was mostly remarkable for his softness. He didn't hand out orders, just told you what you were doing wrong. He knew everything about boxing and nothing about anything else. He was a man completely without character, just someone who was necessary, who had to exist. He didn't say much and he didn't have anything to contribute outside his job.

The woman, who was introduced last despite etiquette, was called Maria Kenrian, and she was a psychotherapist. I'd expected it, but I was still resentful.

"I don't need a PT," I told her, as we shook hands lightly—formally, like fighters touching gloves.

"Everybody needs a PT," said Valerian. "This is the twenty-first century." That was an exaggeration. But for the most part, fighters did need psychotherapy. Sim boxing is something you do with your head and your head has to be in shape for it—not just the motor connections but all of it. The psych aspect is very important. But I thought I was exempt. I didn't admit that I needed PT. I wanted to do it my way. And there was an extra reason that I had to be wary—on paper, Valerian would be paying Dr. Kenrian to help me win. But the real contract might be slightly different. She might be there to make me win his way. I wasn't about to let any fancy mindbender turn me into a plastic imitation of Paul Herrera.

I looked her over. She was in her thirties, with silvery hair curling under at the shoulders. Her face was crisp and hard—pretty, in a way, but pretty like glass or metal, not like flesh. She was an *objet d'art,* not a human being. She didn't look particularly bothered by my attitude but it wasn't exactly lust at first sight. The way she was looking at me I felt like an object too.

"Dr. Kenrian will be here to observe for some time each day until the end of the week," said Valerian smoothly. "After that, you'll fix up appointments between you when it's deemed necessary. Either Curman will drive you into town to see her or she'll come out here—it depends on the way she wants to handle the case."

I didn't bother objecting to the word "case". I just shrugged.

We all moved to one side to look over the equipment.

"It's all new and up-to-date," said Valerian, "but you'll be used to working with all types. There'll be no adjustment difficulties. You start with a big advantage. Thanks to your work you're virtually in full-time training."

I nodded, noting the slight note of irony in his voice. I'd been in training for eighteen years. I just hadn't been allowed to apply it the way I wanted to.

After a shade more preliminary chatter I got into the chair and allowed the techs to begin wiring me up. One of the techs maneuvered the headrest into position and adjusted the seat to fit the contours of my frame, while another began fitting the electroreceptor net over my skull. Each contact had to be made separately, and there were eight electrodes implanted in my skull—four afferent, four efferent. Each one, of course, could carry a vast number of coded impulse-sequences simultaneously—the actual number of organo-metallic synapses was something on the order of sixteen million. Adjusting the set to my convenience was a long drawn-out task, initially. The techs had a lot of very accurate measuring and calibration to do. At the studio I could get loaded up in a matter of minutes, because my personal data was on file, but this was a new ball-game and they were doing a thorough job. There was a little pain. Don't ever let them tell you that having your head wired for cyborg-symbiosis is the easiest passport to an exciting new career. It hurts.

I noticed that Maria Kenrian was hitching up to one of the E-link receivers. Wolff didn't bother—he just wanted to see how the sim was handling. The receiver, of course, had no direct contacts because the resonance induction works across the skull bones, so she was ready long before I was. She wasn't getting anything through, though, because the sim image has to be called up and integrated before the circuit is complete and the miracle of MiMaC begins to happen.

To begin with, they just put up a punch bag. No opponent, programmed or handled. Ira Manuel had made no move to get hooked into the other control unit, and it looked like he was going to have an idle day. He had only come out for the introductions.

I had one last look round the edges of the mask before they switched me in and I had to forget all about the outside world. I abandoned my body while the essential me—the mind, soul, *ka* and so on—became possessed of the sim body. The five-nine, two-hundred pound vehicle which God had issued me was traded in for six-three and two forty-five. All muscle, king-size and powerful.

You'd think that the guy who'd be mentally best equipped

for handling a sim would be the guy who's own vital statistics are six-three and two forty-five, but that's not so. You have to be aware of doing something different, to switch over to a new mental regime. Otherwise you make mistakes—you reproduce in the sim all the stupid habits your own body's lapsed into, and you become confused by the limitations of the sim. Different kinds of possible and impossible are involved.

I moved round the bag, handling lightly and comfortably, hitting out without power, trying to show off my speed and ease instead of burning up the energy carefully programmed into the sim. I felt good—not excited, but pleasant. At home.

After the bag, Wolff put me through my paces with a selection of miscellaneous exercises and feats of strength—the kind of thing you have to do to be super sportsman of the year, all petty tests of coordination and control. It's all a matter of making the best use of the sim's abilities. For me, it was facile. Any one of a hundred Network handlers could do the same—this wasn't where the real difference between one man and the next came in. Any Network hack could beat the super sportsman of the year, but what he couldn't do is control his efforts into one set of skills and potentials well enough to get the absolute maximum out of a sim in terms of one specific set of demands. That takes talent as well as craft.

Nevertheless, they kept me farting about with the play stuff for more than an hour, and they—apparently—didn't get bored.

Eventually, though, when I was beginning to get a little tired, and the sim was beginning to slow down—manifesting all the symptoms of fatigue exactly as if it were a real body—they decided it was time for something better.

Instead of sending Manuel in they used a programmed sim—one that just shuffled around and blocked punches, without throwing any of its own. It couldn't react much, and without a real mind inside it it couldn't get involved. It was really only a glorified punch bag, but it had the advantage of being manipulable. Its reflexes could be turned up, its blocking made much faster, so that over a period of time you had to keep getting more out of yourself in order to keep putting punches through its defense.

I started off slowly, well within myself. I didn't go all out to impress anyone. I treated the shambling zombie with a certain amount of respect.

They turned up the speed, as I knew they would. They were going to test me—to expose a few limitations, find out where work had to begin. I didn't try to turn it into a competition—I was as interested in measuring my performance as they were. I continued to stay within myself, but I continued to put punches through the dummy's defenses until they had the thing up within a thousandth of a second of optimum. By then I couldn't hit it any more but, I was willing to lay odds that Ray Angeli had had to work for months before he had reached that kind of standard. That zombie could have gone fifteen rounds with Herrera and not taken too much punishment.

I was well content with the shape I was in, though I knew I was going to attract some criticism anyhow.

Carl Wolff just condemned it out of hand. "Sloppy," was his sole judgment. He wasn't an easy man to please.

"After twenty years," I said, "it was damn good."

He shrugged.

"There's a good deal more to it than shaping up your reflexes," said Maria Kenrian.

They were still unlocking me from the equipment, and I could do little more than glance sideways at her. She held up the B-link headdress and said, "I'm not talking about what comes over this. I'll need to look a lot longer and harder. But you have other, inevitable problems of attitude. The way your body is geared to respond to your mind has all the wrong assumptions built in. For almost half your life you've been working as a handler in simulation drama, where the priority is looking good. All your actions are deliberately exaggerated, held long enough to show an audience what you're doing. When you throw a punch you're not concentrating on hitting what you're aiming at, but on looking as if you're throwing a punch. You're faking, and you've been faking so long that you're no longer conscious of the fact. There's a world of difference between fighting for real and fighting so that it looks as if it's for real. Fiction always looks more real than reality, because fiction is so self-conscious, whereas reality is slipshod.

"Since you were last in the ring, Ryan, you've become a very accomplished actor. And if you were to go back into the ring tomorrow you'd do so *as an actor*—you couldn't help yourself. You'd put up a show, and you'd lose.

"You suppose that the job you've had these last eighteen years has kept you fit. You think it's given you a better knowledge of handling sims than most boxers, and you think this experience will stand you in good stead. In a way, you're right—it will have kept *certain aspects* of your talent in trim. But what we have to recover is the other aspects—the ones you don't even realize are gone. We have to override some of the assumptions eighteen years have ingrained into your mind. It can be done—but not if you persist in an attitude of quiet hostility and inflexibility. If you continue in the firm belief that you have it all under control, and that it will all be easy, you'll lose. And not only to Herrera— you simply won't get that far. You can't just slip back eighteen years in your life to your younger self—and even if you could, you know that Herrera is no longer the same man he was then.

"If you won't accept all this, then I suggest you watch yourself very closely when you start sparring with Ira. At present, he's a better boxer. He'll give you a rough time for a week or two. Only when we see how fast you improve to beat him can we gauge your chances of recovering the class and skill you once had. You must realize that it isn't automatic. You have your chance now, but you've no God-given right to succeed."

When she finished, I didn't have anything to say. It was all too likely to be true. My self-assurance took a dive, kayoed in round one.

"That," said Valerian, "is what you need a PT for."

"Thanks a lot," I said, my voice congealed and unyielding.

I eased myself out of the chair, with sweat sticking my shirt to my back. I stretched slightly, to get the feel of having my own body back again. I appreciated the tingle of circulation reviving forgotten limbs. Minutes dragged by while the tingle became uncomfortable and I dared not stand in case I couldn't support myself. I felt like I'd had fifteen rounds with Herrera already. It always feels that way when you come out.

My eyes moved from face to face, studying them all, trying to figure out what was behind their patient masks. Only Curman was smiling.

I shrugged slightly. It's never easy.

CHAPTER SIX

Over the next few weeks I gradually settled into a new routine for living. I expected it to be difficult, but certain aspects of it were very easy. When you're pushing forty you don't really expect that you can be uprooted and thrown into a world which is totally alien to everything you've encountered in your past without extreme feelings of dislocation. But it wasn't like that, for several reasons.

For one thing, I never really thought of Valerian's fortress as anything but an alien place. I never made any attempt to "adjust" to it, to "fit in". I just stayed there, and in a way my real life remained back in 3912, just temporarily stored away, in a borrowed suitcase. Secondly, of course, this was something I'd always half-expected. All the time I'd been working as a stunt man at the studios I'd carried around this notion that I was *in transit,* that it was only a way station in my life. I'd never really settled at all. I guess I'd always felt like Cinderella—in the cellar by mistake while my real destiny was to K.O. Prince Charming. I'd even known that Valerian was—or would be, however reluctantly—my fairy godmother. They say that there are only two basic plots—Cinderella and Jack the Giant Killer—and that applies to the way you script your life as well as the way writers script your fantasies.

Anyhow, the old life—the false life—had been easy enough to screw up and throw away. I started anew, without my past hanging round me like a stuffed albatross. There was a whole new structure to my time and my habits and my thoughts, which came ready-made and precisely defined, thanks to Valerian and Carl Wolff.

A new world, off the peg.

For the most part, the life of Ryan Hart mk.III consisted of full days and empty evenings. Wolff and the techs and Ira Manuel took up my days, hustling me through a punishing program calculated to leave me mentally and physically exhausted—and pliable. I only existed, from their point of view, when I was connected to the machine. When they switched off, I retired into electrical oblivion. Occasionally, Wolff would remonstrate with me gently, but he always did so as if I were somehow unreal, like the way some people talk to their cars. There was no human-to-human interaction. I guess the territories in my mind had been pretty clearly demarcated, so that Wolff knew where his jurisdiction ended and Dr. Kenrian's began.

The good doctor evidently believed in not rushing in. She was a real angel. For long periods during the first two weeks she was in attendance while I was being hustled inside the sim, but she did little more than observe through the B-link. She didn't deliver any more speeches, ask any embarrassing questions, or even ask to do the standard psycho-profile tests you have to ham your way through in order to change your job or enlist in the IA. After awhile, I got positively anxious about her refusal to communicate. It's like being in the hospital, with the doctor coming to look you over every day, and then just going away shaking his head morosely. You may only have a bunion but he'll have you convinced it's terminal cancer in no time. I began to suspect hidden depths in my mind.

I had to admit, though, that what she'd said on the first day had a strong element of truth in it. Ira Manuel, who was nothing but a consistent hack fighter, with nothing to distinguish him from the average, did give me a hard time in the ring for awhile. In the first week he was obviously acting on instructions to show me how my cockiness was betraying me because he went after me in a rather more aggressive manner than sparring partners are supposed to do. In this day and age, of course, you can spar as hard as you like, because no one gets injured, but generally you take it easy so as not to lose the edge that real competition gives you. It doesn't pay to punish yourself in training. But Ira took care to punish me.

I didn't hold it against him. I can take a hint. But if you get hit, you hit them back. It doesn't have to be vindictive—it's just the pace the situation sets. Week one he was hurting me, but by the tail end of week two I was hurting him. We threw some pretty hard punches around, and I was reminded sharply of the fact that fighting is for real. Being convinced is half the battle, but it's the quick half. Retraining my subconscious was going to take time.

Valerian came in to watch me a couple of times, early on, but soon dropped the habit. Having roped me in and established me in the schedule he seemed to lose interest entirely. For him, it was now a matter of waiting—waiting until I faced Herrera. The sand that drained through the hourglass in the meantime was just a waste, to him: a slice out of his life, just one of those things you have to keep going through until you come out the other side. Any day his dialyser might clap out or his all-electric heart might give up the ghost, but there was nothing that could be done except wait. I saw him at mealtimes, and though over-the-table conversation was anything but free-flowing I could see his resentment of me and the whole situation slowly growing. The world had condemned him to going through it all, and he wasn't used to being dictated to, even by the inevitable.

He hated me with an awesome, silent fury. But he sat down with me, and ate with me, and passed the salt with a self-control I could almost admire.

Curman always ate by the clock, just as we did, but he was invariably silent as a ghost when his boss was present—just an extra limb for Valerian to command, with no perceptible identity of his own.

Stella rarely turned up on time, though her place was always set. Either she found time completely irrelevant to the business of living or she preferred to avoid her grandfather as much as was convenient. On a number of occasions she came in just as he was leaving. They didn't seem to interact much—they maintained a policy of peaceful co-existence without conflict or companionship. It was as if they were living on different intellectual and emotional planes. Valerian's world permitted such things to happen. It was possible for countless utterly lonely lives to be lived within the shadowed confines of his sprawling house.

I took to reading in the library to occupy a significant percentage of my spare time. I steered clear of the holo, which seemed to absorb most of Curman's free time, and maybe Stella's as well. The opportunity to handle and read the books in the library—printed on a wide variety of types of paper, with no economy measures in evidence—was one I suspected I might never have again. Most of the Valerian heritage—the big house, the grounds, the abundant paraphernalia of wealth and nostalgic style—struck me as being ridiculous and ugly, but the books were different. They were the one aspect of the carefully preserved past that seemed to me to have value.

I excused myself on the grounds that my interest in the books was very different from Valerian's. I was interested in them as devices of communication, while to him they were merely objects. The excuse was almost entirely honest.

It was while I was in the library one night, maybe three weeks after I'd first moved in, that the first faint breath of human contact finally came my way. Stella had become interested enough to investigate me. I was glad to see her. The interpersonal vacuum into which I had been cast was less than comfortable.

I was sitting in the chair that Valerian had occupied the first time I had seen him. She came in, shut the door behind her, and seated herself in the other chair—the one which the old man had offered to me on the night of our confrontation. She made no pretence of being interested in the books, but simply looked at me.

I gave it a couple of minutes, then lowered my book to my lap, keeping it open at the right place with my fingertips.

"I didn't know boxers could read," she said.

"You don't get punch drunk from operating in a sim," I replied.

"You can get killed." She obviously didn't consider it a delicate matter. I didn't know what to say in reply, so I waited for her to begin again.

After a few seconds, she said, "That book has probably remained virginal since it was first acquired. Maybe a hundred and fifty years of unopened, undisturbed bliss. Now you come and assault it. How do you think it feels?"

This approach seemed much more promising. It lacked intensity.

"Profoundly grateful?" I suggested.

"A pig attitude," she said.

I looked at her carefully. She seemed suddenly completely out of place. In the library, in the house, in the world. She looked very small. Remembering all the times I'd seen her previously I could not find one moment in which she'd seemed to be interwoven with the situation or the circumstances. She was living in a kind of cocoon, letting everything flow on around her. A wild card in a carefully stacked deck.

"Tell me," she said, apparently tired of waiting for my move in the exchange of trivial remarks, "what's in it for you?"

"In what?" I stalled.

"You know what," she replied, shortly. "I don't quite see you as a part of it. The others—they all fit in. Common sense says what was in it for them. It was easy to see what they expected to get out of it. Ray, and the one before, *ad infinitum*—they had it all to gain. Boys wanting a boost into becoming men. Full of hope and empty of sense. And even now they're still chasing their moonbeams to the bitter end. But you're not one of them. You're not stupid. So why take the part?"

"Second childhood," I said, easily, trying to resurrect the trivial tone she'd abandoned. "I always wanted to be world champion. There comes a time when you think maybe you did it all wrong and it's time to go back for a second chance. A last fling before existential paralysis sets in."

"You're lying," she said.

"True," I conceded.

"Whatever's pushing you," she said, "it isn't the same kind of thing that pushed all the others. It isn't a wide-eyed hunger for fame and applause. There's something different."

"I want to win," I said.

She waited.

"It's all there is," I told her. "There's no more. I just want to win. That's the whole story."

I thought she was going to call me a liar again, but she didn't.

"Ask Dr. Kenrian," I said. "She must have me analyzed by now."

She shrugged off the mention of Maria's name. "She's just bait," she said.

The statement surprised me. "Why do you say that?" I asked.

"I've seen it before," she said. "We've been through this game more times than I can remember, and I know how it goes. It's part of the package—one of the prizes. It's all a matter of motivation. You're supposed to get hung up on her, get the juice flowing in your glands. It mixes you up, makes you fight a little harder."

I shook my head. "Not this time," I said. "It may be the way they tackle the youngsters, but I don't need that kind of motivation. I don't mix easily. And my glands are subject to rigid discipline."

She didn't believe me. She wasn't a great one for taking statements on trust. I wondered whether there might be a grain of truth in what she said. It was Maria Kenrian's job to get my head right for the fight, one way or another.

"Who do they use to bait the boys?" I asked. "You?"

"I don't play." She said it firmly, perhaps slightly contemptuously.

It was an opening. "Why not?" I asked.

"Why should I?" she countered, reversing the age-old turnabout.

"You tell me," I said. "It's you we're talking about."

"Because it's a farce," she replied. "A hypocritical panto-mime. I hate it."

"I'll believe the last of those reasons," I said.

She had no reply ready for that one.

"He was your father, wasn't he?" I followed up, more gently. "And the old man's only son. Don't you think the feeling that underlies it all is natural?"

"No," she said. "There's nothing natural in it at all. I wasn't even born when my father was killed. All I know about him is second hand. And what they say about him isn't about a real person at all. Just about an idea. That's not natural. I don't think my grandfather even remembers his son. The big grief, the determination to equal the score—all that's synthetic, plastic, a mask he bought in a magic shop.

"I don't believe that my father and my grandfather ever knew one another. I don't believe they liked one another, or ever really met. The part my grandfather is acting was written for him after the event. It helps to keep his strength up—his strength of character, that is. Whatever he pretends to be, he has to be intensely. It's the only way he knows how to live. He's a hard man, made out of stone, claws of pressed steel. He's doing what he thinks he has to do—not for my father but for his own self-respect. He's made Herrera a whipping boy, to take all the punishment he won't take himself. All his sins get shifted, one by one, on to other people. His friends, his enemies, you and me. But Herrera is our figurehead—the representative of all that he wants to destroy. He's the victim in the great ceremony."

"Why tell me?" I asked her. "Do you think I don't have my own ideas about what Velasco Valerian is, and what he's trying to do? Even a pawn can bear a grudge. Do you want me to give up, to refuse to play?"

"I want to know what's in it for you," she repeated. "Why are you helping to keep this thing alive?"

"I'm going to kill it," I said. "Once and for all."

"You can't," she said.

"I'm going to beat Herrera."

"And that's all it takes?"

"For Valerian, maybe not. But it's all I want. Afterwards, I'll be on my own. What happens here is none of my affair."

"I have to live with it," she said.

"That's your problem."

She didn't like that. It made her angry.

"What happened to your mother?" I asked, to steer around the bad moment.

"She couldn't stand it. She left."

"Why didn't you go with her?"

"He wouldn't let me go. He never will. He needs me to prop up his image."

"He can't stop you," I pointed out. "You're over sixteen."

She didn't answer that, because she didn't really have to. Valerian could enforce his will, irrespective of circumstances. He was the great dictator. I wondered what she wanted from me. Not help. Perhaps just the understanding—the understanding that Valerian demanded. Maybe she did want me to get out, to stop playing the game. But she must have known she couldn't end it. And in any case, there was no way she could turn me back.

She went to the door, and left, without saying anything more—without even looking at me again. She'd said her piece, poured out all her half-formed ideas. There were probably no words to express what she really felt.

In a way, she was on my side.

I intended to beat Paul Herrera in such a way that Valerian could get no real kick out of vamping me when I did it. I wanted to beat him calmly, without any animosity. Cleanly, and simply. I thought she might approve of that. It was something—an appropriate gesture. But she wanted so much more. She wanted out, and there was no way. All she could do was wait, and when the old man died she could take the money and run. Wherever she wanted to go.

Or, alternatively, she could take over where he left off. You

don't just inherit money—you inherit the assumptions that go
with it. I felt sorry for Stella.

.

CHAPTER SEVEN

In training, I gradually worked up to the point at which Ira
Manuel could no longer trouble me. I could read his moves and
react in the way that was appropriate to a boxer rather than an
ET taking a dive for the heroes of the Space Patrol. The familiarity of my rediscovered role did not recur overnight, but as it
did come back it brought a complete and safe contempt for Ira
Manuel. He became less useful, and was demoted in importance so far as my program was concerned.

Then Wolff brought in a replacement. At least, I thought at
the time that Wolff was responsible, but maybe not.

The new boy was named Burne Caine. It wasn't his real
name—just something picked for show—but he clung to it as if
he loved it dearly, and we never found out what daddy had put
on the birth registration. Probably something vapid and boring.
There are few Smiths left in today's world of disposable labels.

Caine was by no means the same kind of instrument that Ira
was. Ira had been something dull and unyielding—something
I could sharpen my claws on. We hit one another hard, but we
never really found any true sense of competition.

But Caine had hot blood. He took everything seriously, and
he always looked ready to spit in my eye, inside the sim or out.
He was a teenager, half-Asian and still wearing the livid scars of
a hard past. He was nervous with his hands, and it was easy to
see that translating his fighting into the sim hadn't drained the
tensions out of his body.

I could look at Caine and see Paul Herrera twenty years

earlier. Herrera, like most good handlers, was a guy who'd never had much success handling his own body. He'd never been at home in his own flesh. He'd been a sickly kid growing up in a concrete jungle. He'd had a brain and bad eyesight. He'd had the shit kicked out of him here, there and everywhere. Anything near his size was an enemy. Most kids like that have no option but to wait it out, to grow up into another world—in the meantime staying meek, mild and ready to run like hell. But not Paul. He'd always had the compulsion to fight back, even when it was hopeless. He was more than just a sucker for punishment—he was something of diabolical single-mindedness. He just could not accept defeat, although his whole life and his whole environment were saturated with it. He lost every real fight, but compelled himself to keep going. The fact that he survived to enter the adult world at all had been a minor miracle. Once in it—

And here was Caine, looking at me out of eyes that mirrored the same kind of implacable hatred for everything animate and inanimate.

Caine wasn't there to spar with me. He was there to show me what a real fight was.

The first time we were hooked up together, facing one another in the ring, I knew this wasn't routine. I wasn't ready to go into a Network ring for an officially-recorded fight, but that didn't mean that I was exempt from the fury and the determination of a fight to the bitter end. That was what Caine was for—to push me in a way that Ira Manuel never had.

The worst thing about it was knowing that the kid had his own brand of invincibility. No matter how many times I hit him, he was going to keep coming back, trying ever more desperately to hurt me as much as he could.

Caine had no class. He had very little skill. But he had guts. For three rounds, he hammered his sim, coming in at a pace which had to tire him out in minutes. I was content to defend at first, keeping his jabs and hooks out of my face and body, and just moving round the ring to make him chase me. I tapped him a couple of times, to let him know how easy it was, but made no attempt to hit him hard.

In the fourth, I began to hustle him a bit, out-boxing him all the way. I took a couple of punches that might have rocked me, but traded better ones that should have knocked him groggy. The sim took the physical punishment, but I could almost see Caine shrugging it off. He had a bad case of the "what-the-hell-it-ain't-my-body" syndrome. In a sense, he was punishing himself, though there was no earthly reason why.

The fifth was worse—now he couldn't get to me at all, but he was still chasing and carving with his gloves. I could have hit him at will, but I hesitated. I knew what I was supposed to do. I was supposed to knock him out. I was supposed to knock him out today, and tomorrow, and maybe the next day. It was like spearing fish in a bathtub. He'd take it, again and again, and come back. I was supposed to be cruel. I was supposed to knock hell out of him.

But my mind rebelled, and on the point of laying him out I hesitated. I found myself adrift in the quicksands of doubt. I didn't know what I wanted to do—capitulate with the way I was being maneuvered, or tell them to go to hell.

I had little enough sympathy for the kid, who was worse than a fool, but I didn't want to beat all hell out of him just to make him face that fact.

He kept after me, just as mad, just as heavy as he possibly could. I began to think that by holding off I was hurting him worse than I would be if I took him apart. He knew I was playing games with him. He was still trying to hurt me, trying all the more desperately.

At the end of the round, I said, "That's enough."

Wolff's voice came at me from nowhere. *"Two more."* Not a question, or an instruction, just a statement of the way it was going to be.

"No," I said.

But no voice came back. I couldn't stop it myself—the only way I could switch off the sim was by staging a massive physiological disturbance which would short out the circuit with the emergency cut-out. It's not the kind of thing you can manufacture consciously.

Caine was up and in the ring. I hung back, gloves on the ropes. I could see from his face that he was uncertain, for once. Hesitant. He wanted more. He wanted to win. He just didn't know. He wanted me out in the middle, where he could exhaust himself trying to reach me.

When he knew I wasn't coming he was stranded momentarily.

Then he came after me anyway, bombing in, looking to land good, solid punches before I could get my arms up. Reflexively, my guard came up and I ducked. But the sheer force of his attack carried his blows through.

They took me in the head.

I didn't hit him back. I didn't attempt to crash a fist into his exposed ribs. I just took what he handed out, and then I went down on one knee. A slight touch of nausea from the punches took hold of me, but faded fast.

I looked up into the face of Caine's sim. He was using the white and the pale features were ruddy under the glow of the lights. Sweat was glittering on his forehead. The features were twisted out of their sculpted reality in almost exactly the same way that Paul Herrera twisted them. For a moment, I was left with the illusion that it was Herrera I had been fighting, that it was Herrera who had put me down. I wondered whether I had been intended to fall under that spell right from the start, and be committed by the similarity.

But I hadn't. I remained cool, and I didn't get up.

His eyes told me he wanted to hit me again, and again, and beat me to a simulated pulp.

But he couldn't. The rules wouldn't let him, and a sim can't break the rules. He was as helpless as a baby. I took the count feeling that the whole thing was stupid, irrelevant—a waste of time.

And I began to laugh.

As in the old joke, it hurt when I did.

Back in reality, when they peeled the electrodes from my head, I no longer felt like laughing. I was confused. So was Caine. Even when they had him stripped he just couldn't understand it. He was looking to catch my eye, and I let him. He looked at me as if I were a dead caterpillar in his supper pack. But he couldn't think of anything to say.

It was only then that I noticed Maria Kenrian waiting by the door. She must have come in late. But I didn't need to ask whether she'd seen it all. She'd been eavesdropping on my mind, and she'd done more than simply see it. I suddenly felt angry with her, for the deception and the staginess of the whole affair.

When I was free again she opened the door to the outside world and we strolled out together. It was late afternoon and it was hot and hazy. There were a lot of wasps in Valerian's gardens—there was presumably a nest somewhere near the training unit that the legion of serfs hadn't troubled to destroy—and I waved a couple away as I stepped out into the sunlight.

"You see the point of what happened today?" she asked.

"Not really," I replied. "I think the message got a little garbled." My voice was brittle and bitter, still antagonistic to the whole idea.

"You're screwed up inside," she said. "It's getting in your way. You're thinking about too many things at once, looking at it from too many angles. You're not reaching anything like a fighting pitch because you're perpetually looking over your shoulder to see who's pushing, asking yourself how and why and what the hell."

"It was a farce," I said.

"Of course. But that isn't your concern. All you had to do was go out and beat him—knock him out. But you couldn't do that. You had to hesitate and wonder what it was all about and who was trying to trick you into doing what. You lost that fight half a dozen ways, and it's no good telling me or telling yourself that you could have won if you'd wanted. Of course you could have. But you didn't. You were looking to foul up."

"So?"

"You think it doesn't matter," she said. "You think that this is all a pantomime, and that when you finally get to face Paul Herrera it will all be real, and when it's real it will all be different. *Then* you can win. Perhaps you can. But you *won't*—not unless you can cure your state of mind."

I shook my head. "I like my state of mind," I told her. "I'm entitled to it. It fits me like a glove. I don't want to cure it."

"But you want to win."

"And you think I can't? You think that what's going on in my mind will stop me?"

She didn't say anything for a couple of minutes, probably wanting to make me think about the answers myself.

"I beat him before," I said.

"Do you know how?"

"I hit him harder and oftener than he hit me."

"And do you know *why?*"

"Because I wanted to win."

"And you think that's enough?"

"It was then."

She didn't say anything again, but her answer was written all over her face. *It isn't now,* she was implying.

We had almost reached the house, but as I made a turn to take us round to the nearest door she put her fingertips on my arm and pointed to another way, along a footworn path that led toward the wood via a paved diamond with an ornamental pond. It had goldfish. Also bronze figurines that were mired and patinated. One was a bronze Cupid that had been some ancient humorist's idea of a fountain.

"In those days," she said, speaking quietly, "wanting to win was all there was. You wanted to win—and that was just about the whole story. You didn't question your own decisions, you didn't see anything beyond or behind the business of winning. It was enough to go on, and on—

"But not any more. You're eighteen years older—eighteen embittering years through which you've carried that need to win triumphantly, as if it were the trophy you never got. Carrying it all that way may not have changed it much, in itself, but you've brought it into an entirely new context. It's no longer the dominant force in your mind, it's no longer the focus of your personality and your ambitions. It's a kind of bloody relic of a broken past, and it carries with it a host of conditions and uncertainties.

"If you want to beat Herrera, you're going to have to recover something of that old single-mindedness. You're going to have to put everything else aside. You can harbor your grudge against Valerian, you can try to cheat the mind riders and the system and Network and the world. You can assert your injured pride. Or you can win. But you can't have it all ways."

I reached the edge of the pond a stride ahead of her and pivoted quickly. We ended up facing one another, both standing still. She'd stopped abruptly.

"I'm not a fool," I said to her, softly. "I'm not just a lump of human clay to be molded by you or Valerian, poked and prodded by PT tricks. I can play the game too. I'm good at games. Don't try to tie puppet-strings to my balls."

She stepped sideways smoothly, increasing the distance between us and making me half-turn to keep my eyes on her face.

"Why do you think I brought Caine in?" she asked.

"To get some emotional action out of me. To make me angry or vindictive. To let some of his fire rub off, or bounce off, or—what the hell."

"I brought him to show you the difference between yourself and Herrera. He's the other side of the coin—your mirror image."

"Sure," I said. "Burne Caine and me. Twin souls." I didn't bother to laugh.

"He's everything you're not. And you no longer have anything except what he hasn't got. He's active, and you've become passive. You let the outcome of that fight depend entirely on what *he* did. You did nothing yourself. You sat back in your mind and you evaluated the situation and you worked out how to react—what reaction the situation demanded. You can't fight that way. If you place yourself at the mercy of a situation it will kick your teeth in. It's not the right way—and you must realize that. Your cold, clean thoughts have been a comfort to you these last eighteen years, but they're no good to you in the ring. You're pure and uncut, while Burne Caine is torn to shreds—but he has the one thing that you need. He wants to win and *all else is irrelevant.*"

"That's no way to live," I said—a stupid remark.

"It's the only way to fight," she replied.

I squinted up at the sun—a dull yellow phantom half-hidden in translucent smoke.

"But other things *are* relevant," I said. "They're relevant to me."

"That," she said, "is the problem. The question you ask yourself now is, *How badly do I need the chip on my shoulder*?"

"Caine won today," I said, doggedly, "because he didn't know when to stop. He hit me, and I went down—because there was no point in carrying on. It just didn't matter any more."

"That's exactly right," she said. "And that's exactly why you'll lose again. You'll have a hard ten or twelve rounds, and your opponent will still be standing, worn out but not beaten. You'll see him coming at you again, and you'll start looking in your mind for excuses. What's the point? Does it matter? Why am I trapped here hyping up Valerian, hyping up the world? Why?

"And then you lose."

"No," I said.

"Down you go," she went on. "Because it just doesn't matter *enough.* It's all too heavy to bear—carrying Valerian and the mind riders and your halo and your spirit of callous indifference towards existence in general. All that is too expensive. You can't afford it—not in the ring. The ring is its own little world, and there's nothing beyond its ropes. Your mind has to get inside that microcosm and conform to its laws. You can't stand back outside, and try to stay in the real world as well. Herrera won't."

This time, I was silent. I couldn't even manage a weak disclaimer. I believed her. She was convincing me. There was no earthly way I could know whether it was true or not, but she was convincing me.

She knew it.

"So?" she prompted.

I dropped my gaze from the sky to study the goldfish. They were big, ugly things with patches of silver scale and expressions of utter vacuity. The water where they hung suspended was dull, except where the fountain stirred it up and let the sun shimmer delicately in the droplets.

"So you want to restore my will to win," I said, dryly. "You want to strip away all the paintwork, rip out all the fittings, get back to the basic frame—and then make it into a replica of its old self. Ryan Hart, Mark One—they don't build them like that any more. How do you go about it?"

"That's for you to decide," she said.

"I have a choice?"

"All the choice there is."

"I can choose my own prizes? Plan my own shock therapy?"

"You can co-operate. You can help me find out how to break down that tangled mass of resentment and confusion, help me reach the motivational structure underneath."

"And help you wind me up and set me going. A clockwork toy."

"That's a fool's way to look at it."

"And I'm a fool. Valerian's fool. That's what he wants. He beckons me out from under my stone, after all these years, and he waves his magic wand to wipe out eighteen years and turn me into the kind of pet he always wanted."

"He wants you to win."

"*His* way."

The goldfish opened and closed their mouths, completely passive, completely uncaring. Bone idle and fearless, unaware of the turgid rhythm of their lives, perhaps of life itself.

I spat in the water, and they didn't even swim away.

CHAPTER EIGHT

The next day they put me in the ring again. Wolff was against it, I think, but higher authority called the tune. If Wolff had been the kind of man who took an exaggerated pride in his work maybe he could have had his way, but he was no absolute dictator of circumstance. He let it go.

Maria Kenrian wasn't there. She had left it all up to me, for the time being. She had left the conversation of the previous day hanging limp and unfinished. She was waiting. It was my move.

I knocked the kid clean off his feet in three. I did it quite calmly and with not the slightest hint of malice aforethought. I could even have pretended I was doing it for his own good, but I didn't. I pretended, instead, that I was doing it for mine. It was a clean K.O.—I didn't have to beat him up much to set him up for it.

He was then disposed of. He had made his point—or Maria's point. We washed our collective hands of him and sent him back to oblivion with his fists full of money and his nervous twitch intact. I didn't suppose I'd ever hear of him again. He wasn't good enough to climb off the bottom rung of the ladder and he never would be.

They informed me the same night that I was fixed to fight for real against a steady but undistinguished fighter named Joe Tobias. Valerian had persuaded Network to finance the fight, though it would only be broadcast on channel X at an ungodly hour. I wondered that they didn't want to record it and hire a feeler to dub in my part, but even Network didn't want to set precedents like that. They would be guaranteed a fair audience because I was Valerian's new white hope—the Valerian crusade was something of a public joke, but everyone accepted it as a major source of lovable boxing thrills. The Network controllers knew that I wasn't going to be a good winner, from their point of view, but they were sure of their pitch and they could let me in. One lousy cold fish wasn't going to threaten the whole fry-up. Not now. They might not like me, but they could tolerate me.

Preparation for the fight was no sweat—that is to say, the physical side of it was no sweat. But I worried just a little bit. My favorite psychotherapist made no show—she was content to leave it in my hands. I saw it as a sort of challenge, *How far dare you go before you lose your nerve and capitulate?* I was going to go one fight, at least. I was going to have a long, hard look at doing it my way before I gave her a ticket into my soul, with an option to buy pending the surveyor's report.

She didn't have to be there. I asked myself all the questions she would have asked. I took over her job in her absence. I was stirred up by the ideas that she had introduced into my mind. I gave myself a long hard look in the psyche every time I passed a mirror.

I asked myself how I'd go about it if I had her job. It wasn't an easy question. I wasn't impressed by Stella's unsubtle suggestion that I should be guided gently into infatuation. It wasn't my style. I can dissociate myself all too easily from sexual anticipation and sexual pleasure.

I thought of conditioning, but that was looking at the problem from the arse end. It wasn't that conditioning had to be superimposed but that the conditioning I'd acquired throughout my life as a Network hack had to be removed. It was all the new reflexes—the ideas I'd built into the concept of winning, that ought to go.

If they ought to go.

That, of course, was the most worrying point of all. I wasn't sure that I believed in her purist idea of winning. Not any more.

I wasn't sure that winning in the ring was the only winning I had to do. Surely, I thought, I had to win other battles, other games. I wanted to win against Herrera. I wanted to win against Valerian. I wanted to win against Maria Kenrian. I wanted to win against Network. Add it all up, and it all came down to the same fight.

They say that you can't win them all. But I wasn't satisfied by what people say. I thought there had to be a way out—a way that wasn't Maria Kenrian's way. She had pointed out the simple answer, but simple answers are very rarely right.

I held an imaginary dialogue, in which I defended my lack of emotion against her charges.

The vamps, I argued, live on second hand emotion. The intense feelings they need and love so much are provided for them by a chrome-plated headdress. The dilute feelings—tranquility and happiness—they get in pills. What's left that's theirs? Nothing. They become utterly dependent on Network and the Medical Association. Everything in their lives—in the environment around them and inside their stupid heads—is provided commercially, shaped and tailored to popular demand. What are the vamps except puppets? What do they think or feel that comes from themselves and not from some machine or some chemical? What are they but ciphers in the grand scheme of the human world, no more real than the images in the holo? But I'm not like that. I have individuality. I am what I am, and I intend to protect that. I don't intend to unhappen the events, the feelings, the meaning of eighteen years just so I'll be a better image in the sim, just so I can be packaged as a consumer product, just so I can win with a thrill.

In the imaginary dialogue, she was unintimidated. She had the answer tucked up her sleeve. She knew me that well.

Very good, she replied, sarcastically. Humanity, hang thy head in shame. Ryan Hart will diagnose the social sicknesses of the modern world. *He* is a hero. He doesn't use the E-link, and maintains his emotional independence, his emotional integrity.

But where is it, Ryan?

Where is this rich, self-sustained emotional life you are able to lead thanks to your rejection of the consumer product? What is there to recommend your emotional existence? Is it beautiful, unique, aesthetically magnificent? Where is your own joy, that is so superior to the custom-made variety? Is your home-made happiness so much better than the pills? Does it even exist? How, exactly, are you such a wonderful advertisement for psychic independence? Who is impoverished—the vamps, whose emotional wealth is purchased off the peg, or you, who feel hardly anything at all, most of it bitter?

In a real dialogue, I would be unperturbed by such comments. I would laugh at them. I would manufacture a suitably witty reply, or simply rule them out of court with a gesture. But inside, you can only say something along the lines of, *very clever, but it doesn't get us anywhere, does it?*

And it doesn't.

That's the trouble.

Despite it all, I went into the ring for the first time in half my life with my mind unbent. I carried into the sim all the legacy of my latter days. It was a test—an experiment.

I was nervous as I guided the sim out from the corner. A wholly irrational apprehension gripped my guts—mostly below the belt. I resented it, because there was no need for it and because I couldn't understand it. Also because it was going out to a hundred thousand viewers. It wasn't private. It wasn't something I could keep confined. It was being sucked out of my soul and cast to the winds, tossed to the scavengers.

I couldn't see the meter from within the sim but I guessed that well over sixty percent were riding me. I wouldn't be far short of the proportion that Herrera carried in his fights. Nobody could really fancy Tobias. I wouldn't be fighting him if he had any real chance. I was favorite to win comfortably, not on the strength of my past performances, which were so deeply buried by the years as to count for nothing, but on the strength of my job as a stunt man. In the pre-fight publicity, Network copy-writers had made a big thing about the possibilities of talent being transferable. They hadn't been able to build me up as a fountain of joy so they were making a puzzle out of me, stirring up intellectual interest. I guess the marks probably fell for it. You can sell anything to anybody. Once.

Tobias was a deceptive boxer, with a good line in change of pace. Half the time he was wanting to get on with it, hurrying in to spray punches and always looking like he might cause trouble, and the other half back-pedaling, trying to lure some action out of his opponent. He always gave the impression of being more dangerous than he really was. He was not famed for punching power, and people he beat rarely took a brutal hammering. They just got harassed into submission.

He wasn't too easy to hit, and he didn't mind taking punishment—he, too, like many second raters, was a victim of the it-ain't-my-body syndrome. It ain't, but you have to believe that it is in order to get the best out of it. He'd been brought along fairly carefully by his backers, but they knew by now that he was never going to make them any real money. They were putting him in today knowing he was on a bummer, but hoping he was ready for a long twilight, putting up noble performances against ambitious youngsters for pin money.

I'd decided beforehand that there was no virtue in show, and no point at all in messing about. Right from the first moment I would be addressing myself to Paul Herrera—he was what it was all about. I wanted to start spelling out a message to Herrera with every punch.

So, apprehension or no apprehension, I went out to attack. I went to chase and find Tobias, and I did it. When he came forward, I fought fire with fire, when he went back I gave him no rest. The first round was punishing, and I felt him falter before the end. In the second, and again in the fourth, his determination came fluttering up inside him. For a minute or so he looked capable. But each time he could not sustain himself. He could make nothing of it. He wilted.

With every round he inched closer to defeat.

I didn't lose a round out of the first seven, and in the eighth he went down for good. I can't honestly say that I knocked him down—I think he just faded out from a sense of despair. I hit him with a left hook when he was slightly off balance and he just didn't find the motive force necessary to drag himself back off the canvas. Convinced of the pointlessness of it all, he just lapsed into mental turmoil and stayed crumpled.

It was an easy, untroubled, impressive victory. Curiously, though, the quivering in my belly was still there once he was down. I'd stopped feeling it during the fight, but it was there, in abeyance. As soon as I was still again it took hold of me. Apprehension. Anticipation. Not fear, but a sense of impending events whose uncertain outcome was manifest as a vacillation in the determination to go forward and meet them.

I wasn't expecting a round of extravagant congratulations when the fight was over, and I didn't get one. Carl Wolff signaled his satisfaction in his usual taciturn and unexcited fashion. Valerian hadn't come to the studios but I knew he'd be hooked in at home, not feeling particularly delighted but fairly content that I was on the way. Dr. Kenrian was there when I came out of the machine, having turned up late and unobtrusively, as per usual, but she didn't have anything to say beyond token acknowledgement of the fact that I'd won.

I wondered, briefly, about Stella. I couldn't make a guess as to whether she was in the habit of watching—or even hooking into—her father's avengers, or whether she'd make an exception in my case. I didn't suppose I'd find out.

But there was one man there who wanted to tell me that I'd done a great job, and that was Jimmy Schell. We met him in the studio, and though it looked accidental I was pretty sure that he'd contrived it. I was slightly surprised that he bothered to make it seem like a coincidence, but I guess he still had little or no confidence in himself.

We shook hands, and he expressed his stammering surprise at the way I'd turned up again. The question he didn't ask was, *why didn't you tell me?* I hadn't an answer, and I almost felt guilty about it. When I'd talked to him before, I'd worn a false face. I'd never so much as hinted that I had been a fighter and intended to be again—not even when he had asked me about the Herrera-Angeli fight.

He was working regularly now—small parts, but enough to make a living with a little icing on top. He was still going up. I wished him well and he promised to look out for my next fight. He was a fan. I knew he'd hook in. I didn't like the idea of his vamping my mind, but I didn't want to tell him I didn't like it. To him, it came naturally.

I was only half pleased by the enthusiasm in his voice and his manner. I knew that he was likely to be a maverick. The general reaction could well be hostile—it hadn't been much of a contest from any point of view, least of all the vamp angle. I expected something of a hammering from the free press.

I wasn't disappointed.

The papers were lying in wait at breakfast the next morning. The fight hadn't been important but it had provoked enough interest to warrant giving it space in just about every sheet.

Most of the comments were brief, and if not exactly abusive were far from complimentary. Nobody read anything out loud, but I knew that they all had a pretty good idea of what they said. Even the waiters.

Strangely, it was Valerian himself who was anxious to know my reaction.

"You didn't win many friends," he said, snidely—failing to keep the edge out of his voice.

"I won the fight," I reminded him.

He tapped a couple of the papers. "Not in here you didn't. Not really. To them, it was a joke. They don't say so, but they suspect a fix. They couldn't see that it was honest—you didn't give them any reason to think so."

"If they think honesty is an emotional orgy they're crazy," I said. "Those bastards are just consumer panders, wanting to rearrange the world the way it looks best from inside a head-dress. That's how they sell papers."

"It's how they sell fights," he said. "It's their money. They pay you and your opponent and the techs."

"You pay me," I said.

"They pay *me*," he retorted.

I shrugged that off. "The public wouldn't know an honest fight if they saw one," I said. "They don't want honesty—they want kicks. They're in it for spectacle, not for sport. They only want to pretend it's real. But they can't have it all ways—it can't be real and fake as well. If you want to hire a writer to script the title fight, hire one. Buy Herrera and a first class feeler to act it for you. But if you want a boxer, don't try to tell me that I have to act up so as not to attract dirty sneers about fixing."

"It's still the public that pays," he said.

"So okay," I said. "The best man has to win. I'm the best fighter. Herrera's the best feeler. The audience wants Herrera, but under the rules—under the conditions laid down by the men who believe in competition and not in comedy—it's going to be me that wins it. You can whine, but you still can't have it both ways."

He went back to eating, his dignity intact. He didn't have to win arguments at his own table. He could just cancel them out of his consciousness. It was his world.

The slight tension drained out of the atmosphere, and I re-directed my attention to scanning the reports.

I was surprised to find that there was one which wasn't hostile—either that or its hostility was sublimated into an invisible irony. It was by a man named Sacchetti, writing for a sheet that probably had an anti-Network axe to grind.

It could be, said the article, *that the neurotic overkill to which our innocent senses and feelings are subjected by the current style in boxing may be tuned down in the near future. It may be that we shall be offered the opportunity to recover a more refined sense of values—perhaps an old fashioned stoicism according to which emotional outbursts are regarded as signs of personal weakness. A new brand of unresponsive, stiff-lipped heroes may soon be launched by the shapers of men. Perhaps such a move is long overdue. Perhaps we may even see the infu-*

sion of some of the skill and character of classical boxing into a simulated sport which has so far been notable only for its brutality.

"Now him," I commented, "I like."

"He's the court jester," said Valerian, barely glancing at the paper and recognizing it from its typeface. "The establishment's pet cynic."

"You think he doesn't mean it?"

"On the contrary," said the old man. "He believes it all too seriously. He wouldn't be amusing if he wasn't grotesquely sincere. But he's only the lone voice who confirms the majority belief by presenting the unpalatable alternative. Even his style is the sort of fancy glibness readers love to take exception to."

"I bet he loves you too," I murmured. I caught Curman's eye but there was nothing in his gaze but calculated blankness. There was not the faintest aura of an opinion about him. He had watched the fight, I felt sure. Hooked into me. He might even have appreciated it.

After breakfast, it was straight back to work. Time marches on and so did the great crusade. Joe Tobias was just one step on the way, and there were plenty more to come.

CHAPTER NINE

A couple of days later I saw Stella again. I was still spending time in the library even though I'd become bored with the books—saturated with their antiquity and no longer fascinated by their feel. Reading the words I still enjoyed, but they felt so remote and so unconcerned. The ideas, as well as the objects which contained them, were stained by the dust of time, alien things in a world which used different instruments for the same purpose. In spite of it all, however, I still found the library the best place for a psychological escape from the heavy, morbid atmosphere. I had all but abandoned going into town, for whatever reason, and was slowly sinking down into the rut Valerian and Wolff had dug for me.

Apparently, my fondness for the library was accepted and approved of by the household, and it was acknowledged as my bolt-hole, my private space. No one ever bothered me there, except Stella, who came to find me. Even she had something of the attitude of an invader.

"Well?" she demanded peremptorily. "You know what you're in for yet?"

"The same as always," I told her.

"You still want to be champion."

"Pretty ridiculous if I changed my mind now, wouldn't it be?" I said. "Do you expect me to have a sudden revelation—hear the call? Decide that all these years I've been looking at the wrong stars? Should I just throw away my entire life?"

"Try another one," she said.

"It's not as easy as that. We only have one each."

"Suppose," she said, carefully, "you lose."

"I won't."

"That's a coward's way to answer," she said. "A refusal to face probabilities. That's not you speaking, it's a defense mechanism. You know you could lose. You must have thought about it."

I'd thought about it all right.

"Well then," I said, trying to keep it light and breezy. "Like Angeli and all the rest. On to the ex-Valerian scrap heap. Or maybe further—all the way back to 3912 and the kiddy-thrills. I won't be short of a job, or a life. I can just put my old habits back on and continue wearing them. There's lots worse off in the IA and the Social Services."

"And grandfather?"

"He'll find another last chance. The shock won't kill him. I don't know that anything ever will. He's tough. He'll just rewrite the screenplay for his declining years. From a man like that there's no way to steal such things as hope. Herrera may crack before Valerian does."

"You don't believe that," she said.

"How should I know what to believe?" I replied, carelessly. "I only work here. Just passing through."

"I'm not," she said. "It's my life."

"I'm the last person to come to for advice about how to live it."

"I don't want advice," she said. "I want to know where I'm up to. If you fail, where are we?"

"Since you put it like that," I said, "I guess in my secret heart of hearts I think I'm the last of the last chances. He blames me for what happened as well as Herrera, and this, finally, is the main feature. In putting me up against Paul he's trying to tie his whole life up with a pink ribbon. He's reached the end. If I win, he'll hate me as fiercely as he ever hated Herrera, but he'll enter it in his book as a victory. If I lose—well, I guess he loses too. Once and for all. Maybe it *will* kill him, or maybe he'll find his way on to a whole new existential wavelength. Either way, it'll be over. For him, for you."

She was silent for a few moments. I wondered why she came to me. Maybe she couldn't work it out for herself. Maybe the gulf between her and Valerian was uncrossable, unfathomable.

"I watched you the other night," she said.

"And?" I prompted.

"You were so cold," she said. "I didn't understand."

So she'd done more than watch. "It's the way I am," I said.

"It's cruel," she stated.

"Why?"

She waved a hand in the air, groping for the words. "If you were angry, excited—all the hitting and the hurting would be natural—in context. It would all make some kind of sense. But your way, it seems cruel. Callous. Hurting just for its own sake."

I shook my head. "Not for its own sake," I said. "Not at all. You have it backwards. It's when a man is excited by what he's doing, committed to it, involved with it—that's when sport becomes cruelty, when the element of viciousness and barbarity comes in. But I don't enjoy hitting anyone. I do it because I'm good at it, because it's a contest."

"But what you're doing is still the same," she said. "You're still hitting someone, still hurting them. Removing the motive from barbarity doesn't make it civilized. It just leaves it without a reason—pointless barbarity."

"You don't understand," I told her. "You look at the fight and you see two men hitting one another. I guess in this day and age that's natural—that's what the vamps see and it's what they want to see. They just like the emotional charge that goes with the violence and they don't understand how much more to it there is.

"But there's an aesthetic quality in boxing. It's a sport, and it's a skill. It's a ritual, demanding that each man get the best out of his abilities. Rituals are something we need, to confirm our identities, to let us know who and what we are. A lot of the devotees of the old sport thought that sims would destroy the element of identity in the sport by making all men start equal, but they were wrong, because starting equal doesn't mean starting identical. There's still skill and style, and getting the utmost out of a sim body is even more difficult than getting the best out of your own. The fighters know that. Even Paul Herrera knows that there's far more to it than beating up the other guy. It's the audience—the mind riders—who can't and won't understand that there's more to winning than the display of brute force."

"Have you ever considered," she asked, "that the audience might have it right and that you might have it wrong?"

"I know what I do," I said.

"And you try to cheat the audience. If you don't do what they want, that makes it all right. It squares your conscience."

"I don't have a conscience."

"Suppose," she said, slowly, "that they make you into what they want you to be. Suppose they make you into a substitute Herrera."

"They can't do that!"

"No? How many minds are there inside yours during a big fight? A hundred thousand. A million. All over the world—and you don't feel the pressure. You don't feel that they can do anything to you. You think they're just passengers."

"That's the way the link works," I reminded her.

"Is it?" she asked. And even though she was talking nonsense there was something in her voice which threatened me. She was trying to retail an old nightmare—mind control via MiMaC. Brain washing, mind distortion, change of personality, Jekyll and Hyde. When vultures settle on a corpse it becomes vulture-meat, no matter what it might have been before. The parasite absorbs the host, and the host's flesh becomes parasite flesh. The virus invades a cell, and the cell is converted to the production of virions. The integrity of the body can break down under a whole host of stimuli, go mad and lose control of itself, become cancerous. And what of the mind? How secure are its walls, how absolute is its structure? When you let in the riders, you surrender yourself to demonic possession. How can any one say that they come through it all unchanged, unsullied, unaffected? How can anyone say that the riders in your mind don't even leave their smell behind?

When Stella was gone, I was still looking for answers. From every side the assault was coming. There was no way to turn without running into someone's challenge, someone's accusation. I wished I could believe it was all a PT plot to undermine my self-confidence, that everyone came with a roster of questions prepared. But I didn't believe that.

I could have shrugged it all off, dismissed it all as irrelevant, settled back into perfect faith in my own aims, my own abilities. But I had to admit that I didn't have such perfect faith. I never had. The only perfect thing I had, untouchable by fate, was my will to win.

I was fixed up for another fight within a fortnight. Then another, and another.

One by one, I disposed of a trio of young hopefuls looking to get a significant start in life. They would all have other chances—nobody expects you to win everything right from the start. In the meantime, they were convenient cannon-fodder. I was never really extended and no fight went the distance.

But we all knew that it was just play—strictly for the record. It was a matter of the quantitative accumulation of wins, to build up my putative reputation as a hard man, a genuine contender. It was for publicity purposes as much as for anything. It was trivial.

Then came the first real fight, against a boxer of good quality. For this one, the pressure came on. Maria Kenrian stepped from the shadows back into the limelight of my life, reminding me by her continual presence of all the things she stood for. This one, she believed, was going to show me the light—it was going to make clear to me just how much I needed the ministrations of a first-class angel.

Again, the apprehension. Again, the determination to attack, to take my courage in both hands and go in to do what I could do, alone and unaided.

But this time, I couldn't just waltz through the first half dozen rounds, stacking them up to my credit like Valerian's servants stacked plates.

It was tough—a genuine contest. I was hustled, and I was hit. I was called upon to produce more power and energy than naturally flowed into my fists. I was called upon to find extra, and keep finding it. Not the kind of extra strength and coordination and fighting style I'd had to call back into the ring against Ira Manuel—that was just something I'd lost and had to find again—but something more. I was in fresh territory, pushed out of my natural depth for the first time.

I tried hard not to lose sight for the merest second of precisely what I was doing. I worked hard, in the sim and in my mind. I never once lost any semblance of control over either. For a while, the fight looked even, but as early as the third I was conscious of a certain superiority. I was a shade better. It wasn't easy making that superiority tell, making a margin of effort between us and keeping that margin widening steadily as rounds went by, but I did it.

It was like running uphill—the further I went the harder and the more punishing it got, but I edged ahead early and he was never catching up. After eleven he began to get desperate, to rush himself, overcommit his moves, and I began cutting him to pieces. He was on the floor in the twelfth and he took the count in the penultimate round.

It was a good win, and it confirmed me as a fighter of class. It made me into an eventual contender, and the way that Valerian was rushing it made me into a man who was likely to climb into the ring with the champion at the earliest possible moment. The press and the audience still didn't like me, but their hostility was being dissolved by a torrent of chatter. The public relations angle of their work began to take over from the opinionating.

Just one month after that crucial fifth fight my final program was arranged. One more medium-sized bogey to dispatch, and then Herrera. The dates of both fights were fixed, although the second was conditional on my winning the first.

I was surprised—not by Valerian's hurry but by Herrera's willingness to cooperate. Generally, he let a long gap go by between fights these days. It wasn't that he needed the time, but that his image did. Network needed a long lapse to keep the vamps hungry and to do a careful cosmetic operation on the probabilities pertaining to the next fight. They always had to make Herrera's invincibility look cracked, to show that each and every challenger had a measurable chance. Even a massacre has to look like a contest in the public eye.

A manufactured myth needs careful and constant maintenance.

But this time Herrera wanted to fight. He wanted to take me early. Network was willing to let him, though they might have preferred to give it a little more time. Herrera was anxious to have me out of the way, and so—for different reasons—were they.

It wasn't that Herrera was frightened of me. He knew as well as I did that the result of the fight we'd had eighteen years ago didn't matter a damn in today's world. It would be two different fighters in the ring this time. But it wouldn't be two different men. What Herrera wanted—and what made him hurry—was his revenge for that solitary defeat. Like Valerian, he wanted to wipe out an insult, and the fact that eighteen years and more had passed only meant that there was no reason to drag his feet now. He had been given the opportunity to redress the balance, and he was ready to grab it at the earliest possible moment. Herrera had a long memory, and in his mind he still had a way to go in paying the world back for the agonies of his youth. He was still a sensitive man.

Once the schedule was settled, my training program was stepped up. To keep me under pressure through the weeks until the big crunch Wolff imported a new sparring partner—a man who could probably get as much out of me in the ring as any other boxer short of the champ himself.

Ray Angeli.

I was surprised to see him. He had a lot of money to make

yet, despite having been demolished by Herrera. A few more wins, careful management, and he would be in the top bracket of the big league. He had vamp appeal, he had skill. So what if he wasn't the world's greatest? There can only be one at a time, and Ray had a long life ahead of him. He'd have more chances, and in the meantime he could cut himself a big slice of the cake. Valerian's money wasn't behind him anymore but there had to be managers queuing up to sign him on.

But instead, he was back in the game. He was a spare in a new operation. Sure, he'd be well paid, but in his shoes I'd have been thinking about my pride.

It didn't take long to find out why he was back. He was *infected.* Somehow, it had all got through to him. It had eaten into his skin and into his heart. He was still thinking, months after his big night, that the one thing of importance in the world was seeing Herrera beaten—not necessarily beating him, but seeing him beaten. Valerian had screwed his head, twisted him somehow. Poor Ray had lived with Valerian and been a part of the crusade for long, long months, and it had all taken hold of him. He had got involved with it. And he still felt at home in the game. He wanted to help me.

He put me through my paces inside the ring, really forcing me through some pretty tough work. Outside the ring, though, he didn't stop. He was still trying to corner me, always trying to get through my guard and hit me—with words, with arguments, with regrets, with advice. It was almost enough to make me scream. Most times, I got away. The house was a refuge—he was no longer the golden boy and he was out with Wolff and the other hirelings—but I knew there couldn't be any real or permanent escape. It was just one of those things that have to be faced. Someday I was going to have to sit still and let him pour out his bitter soul on to my lap.

Eventually, on a day off when I felt so detached from life in general that it seemed I wouldn't mind if World War Ninety-Nine broke out, I agreed to go along with him on a trip into the mountains. The idea was to get—so he said—some clean air and a look at a different world. Wolff declined an invitation but Stella found out and opted in—which meant that Curman was assigned to us as well, because Valerian apparently didn't approve of his granddaughter running round loose, especially in the kidnap season.

I was assigned the front seat, beside Angeli, by a kind of conspiracy of presumption. He talked at me for mile after mile after mile. All the way. He kept his eyes on the road, but his hands were never still on the wheel. They kept wandering to reinforce the points he was making.

"You can beat him," he assured me. In fact, he seemed to assure me of that at the beginning of eighty percent of his paragraphs. It was his premise, his jumping-off point for rhapsodies and fantasies of method and theory.

"I couldn't quite crack him, you see," he explained. "But he can be cracked. And once he is, he's just meat like anyone else. It seems to me he hasn't got quite his old edge—like there's a seam which has been taking all these years of strain and could open any time. Maybe in five years I could take him myself—right now I haven't the experience. But I ran him close and you can follow up, you can take up where I left off and you can break him. For a long time when I was in there with him it was all even. And I began to feel him—you know what I mean—*feel* him taking it in, going back on his reserve tank. Just that little bit extra is all it needs. Do like I did—conserve your strength, don't let him hit you too hard too often—that's your style, I know. If you can do that, hang on in like me, stay with him or ahead of him, keep the tally guessing, I think he'll run out of gas. Twelve, maybe fourteen, he'll go up in smoke. Nothing left. Important thing is not to give, not to crack yourself—but you won't, because you're not the type to give. You're too tough for him. I see you got an edge when we're in the ring. You can take me, you can take him."

I listened. I listened to it all.

I remembered sitting and hoping this fatuous creep could beat Herrera. I prayed for him to do it. But that's sim fighting for you—you never get to see the guy inside the machine. All you see is his image.

"Maybe someday," he said, "I'll come and take the title from you."

Thanks a lot, I didn't say. Thanks for the thought, if such it can be called.

As testimony to the power of a myth, Angeli had a certain fascination. He was roped and tied by ideas which would confine him until the end of his days—unless he got a new revelation in the meantime.

Someone—a whole crowd of someones, including himself—had hammered switches in Angeli's mind until they were sealed closed forever, barring cross-circuits in the brain. Herrera had to be beaten—next time. Had to be. He had no regard for logic—there always had to be a way to do it, a way it could be done. There was always a new formula, a new plan—a recipe for achievement. Racehorse trainers operate on the same kind of basis with regard to slow horses. Every time a nag comes back looking like a tired dog, sweat all over and feeling the whip marks on its arse, beaten out of the finish for lack of speed, class and spirit, there's the trainer explaining to the owner that the race was slowly run. It had a bad draw, it had the wrong jockey, it needs blinkers, it was the way he didn't eat his oats last night. It's never the fact that the horse is a loser. Never. That's the one thing the owner doesn't want to know, doesn't want to hear. It always has to be circumstance.

So there was Angeli, talking to himself *via* me. Every time he found a new word, a new angle, a new excuse, it poured out again. Every time he said, "You can beat him" he meant, "I could have beaten him". He meant, "He can be beaten". He meant anything except, "I lost", "I'm a loser", "He's too good", "He beat me".

Ray Angeli was a tangled man. And yet—he could box.

He had looked good. The vamps drank their fill from him. Losers thrive on illusions. Excuses off the peg, filed and cross-indexed, a logic to support every conceivable event. His intentions were good, of course.

The road to hell is paved with good intentions, and each one has its loser sitting right on top of it, saying, "Where I went wrong was here. If—"

If—

Slowly, the words tumbling in my ears became meaningless. I listened to the sounds, divorced from their meanings. I turned off the language and listened to the stupid, fumbling rhythm.

It was good to get right up into the mountains. I'm no nature lover but I love height. The great stands of green trees don't inspire me at all—they're alien, hopelessly and irredeemably, so far as people who are born and live their lives in a matrix of concrete cages and arterial roads are concerned. But the faces of rock above the tree line—that's something else. On a murky day even the snow on the caps looks as gray as the grime which dresses the crowns of the capstacks and the twilit towers. That's beauty—the reflection of man in nature.

Even today, in the second Age of Enlightenment (or the third, or the fifth, depending on the brand of your pocket calculator) they still champion the beauty of the untouched, unspoilt, unpolluted, unadorned. But that's an archaic view—the romantic syndrome, the aesthetics of fake nostalgia. To me, and to any authentic child of today, there can be nothing intrinsically pleasing about a tree, or a flower, or a carefully-conserved deer with a government-protection tag in its ear and a medical history in some bureaucrat's filing cabinet. No one, bar the self-deluding, can see anything clean or pretty in the round of nature with its thousand parasites and diseases, the biochemical pollution of its scents and pollen dust and its leaking sap. The hell with spring and hurricanes—sulfuric acid rain is clean, and it purifies. That's the sense of values appropriate to the real world, no matter what fantasy land you believe in up above the clouds.

But as I said, losers live on illusions. So do the rich.

Stella got a kick out of it—and, I think, Curman too. Curman was innocent enough to enjoy the things he was supposed to, and clever enough to take them as they came.

I wanted to talk to Stella, but I never got the chance. She didn't seem interested in people at all—not for a while. She hardly even looked at me—or at Ray Angeli. She had said that she liked Ray, but the liking obviously hadn't cut deep. Like Curman, he was relegated to being part of the human furniture of her immediate environment. I don't think he noticed. Or maybe he just didn't allow it to show.

We ate out at a roadhouse that was full to the seams with aging participants in the great nostalgic dream. They were all bubbling with love of the woods and maintained an ostentatious piety in their communion with Eco-God and his unspoilt angels. Come back Pan, all is forgiven.

If they crucified Christ tomorrow there'd be a million and a half people walking on Washington to petition against cutting down a tree to make the cross.

By the time we got back, night had fallen, and as we came down into the city we could see the Valerian estate as an enclave of shadow in a metropolitan corpus that was blazing with atom-fed electric glory. A cast in the eye of civilization.

CHAPTER TEN

And the next day, the sky fell.

It had been hovering a long time.

"I want you to take some tests," said the good doctor.

"PT tests?"

"Emotional reactivity tests, situation resistance, psychophysiological integration. You know the line."

"Why now?" I wanted to know. "Why not in the beginning?" I was manifesting what the PTs call "suspicion and hostility" toward the idea of undergoing what they considered to be the A-1 route to self-repair.

"You know how we do the standard tests," she said.

"You sit the subject down in the middle of a sim projection and then throw in giant spiders and naked ladies. The poor sap gets switched from scene to scene in a matter of seconds and gets thoroughly confused and frightened. A headdress taps the echoes in his brain. When you let him out you tell him which of his mental washers need replacing and give him an estimate for a whole new gearbox. Then he pays over half the credit he'll earn in the next thirty years. You bung him back in the sim, and he sits through an hour a week taking passive part in horrible and embarrassing situations until he's a nervous wreck. Or, to use the correct jargon, sane."

She ignored the greater part of this lucid account and said, "And you know why I couldn't give you the standard tests."

"Sure," I said, deflating myself just a little. "They wouldn't be any good. I spend all my working life in sims—not just sitting in them but *inside* them. I don't get confused or frightened or embarrassed. I've been called upon to attempt rape with the most wonderful naked ladies the computer can produce and I've been some of the nastiest spiders. My reactions wouldn't exactly be—what d'you call it?—*normal*."

"And so," she said, "I've devised some tests tailored to your particular requirements."

I didn't like that idea, though I should have seen it coming.

"I'd have to be wired up to take these tests, I suppose?" I asked, soberly. I'd given up being a facetious churl for the time being.

"Yes."

MiMaC, apart from being a breakthrough in the management and supervision of mechanical production, a revolution in entertainment and a godsend to military training and planning—plus a hundred other applications in just about every field of human endeavor which can put up the money—provides scope for the most effective and ingenious tortures man—or woman—can devise. If I allowed myself to be hooked into a sim situation with neither knowledge nor control of what was going to happen to me therein, I'd be putting myself into a situation of total vulnerability. There are disadvantages to having wires in your head.

"I'm not playing those kinds of game," I told her. "No way."

"Think about it," she said. "It's not to satisfy my own morbid curiosity or to indulge a hypothetical streak of sadism. I want you to find out what your psych profile looks like. I want you to understand better how you tick. It isn't pleasant to go through these tests, trying to identify what scares you, what you don't like, what your idiosyncrasies are. It's stripping you more naked than anyone wants to be. But if you want any measure of command over your state of mind—and you'll need that command for the life-prospectus you've drawn up for yourself—it's something that has to be done. You can no longer afford the luxury of not being able to look at yourself and see more than a face."

"There are other ways," I said.

"Name three."

"Intellectual honesty?"

"You think you've gone through life without ever telling yourself a lie, without ever concealing the truth from yourself?"

I guessed not. But—

"I don't know what you have cooked up for me, but it has to be tough to break through my conscious knowledge that everything in a sim is fake. I don't know how you intend to soften me up so that I'll react, but however you want to do it I won't like it. And I won't go through with it. I don't care whether you're trying to help me or destroy me, I'd rather stay the way I am."

"Nobody can change that except you."

"Don't talk garbage."

"I mean it. I'm not going to put pressure on you. I only want to put you on the horns of a dilemma. I just want to find out how you can turn yourself from a loser into a winner, and I want to tell you how to do it. From there, it's your own decision. You can act, or you can take your chances."

"You still think I'm a loser?"

She looked at me steadily. "I can tell you one thing you're afraid of right now," she said. "And that's being a loser."

I shrugged. "So okay. I don't like the dark either. All kinds of things scare me. I could make out a list—or tell you all about my favorite nightmares."

"The things that scare people most," she said, "are the things they won't admit they're scared of. And in any case, the spectrum of your fears is only something we need to know about. The more important thing is your spectrum of hates. Fear is negative—it can make you a loser but eliminating it doesn't make you a winner. Hate is the other way round—it's hate that gets the best out of you."

"I don't accept that."

"That's precisely the problem."

"Very smart," I complimented her. "Very glib. But it makes no difference. I know damn well that your best interests and my best interests could never get together on a casting couch to make beautiful music. Whatever you want to find out I'm happy enough to keep secret. I can get by."

"I'll show you the test first," she said. "You can watch it played through in the holo from outside, as a spectator. No surprises, no tricks. The way you get softened up to heighten your sensitivity and increase your reactivity is simple enough—just a few minutes SD. Not enough to hurt. You have to remember that it's in no one's interests to have you get hurt. You have a fight next week and you have to win. After that, there's another fight, which you have to be ready to win. We want you in peak shape for those fights, and this is supposed to help you, not half-kill you. You can't lose anything by knowing the alternatives."

"I don't want to do it," I said, flatly.

"Nobody wants to do it," she replied. "Not ever. But mostly they do. It's an accepted fact of life. If you like, take it as a challenge. Fight against the program, try to beat the tests."

I thought about it. In a sense, it *was* a challenge. It was a deliberate challenge to my self-confidence and self-containment. I'd mentioned intellectual honesty, but if I were really intellectually honest I'd have nothing to fear in the tests. Sure, you ought to have privacy in your own head, but privacy is a limited thing, constantly eroded by the circumstances of everyday life. Other people can always see into your soul. It's one of the facts of life.

In addition, there was the fact that if she really wanted to take liberties with my mind the opportunity was there virtually every day. It would be no sweat for her to switch me off Wolff's program and into her own. The only OFF switch I had in the sim was the physiological emergency. You're all alone in unreality, and you can't run away if the rules won't let you.

I knew she didn't want to burn my mind—only warm it up a little. And she was right in saying that she couldn't do anything by force. Valerian and his hirelings wanted to add something *to* me, not build a replacement.

In all likelihood, taking her test wouldn't bother me too much. It might even be interesting. I could make it into a test of my own—a test to see how cool I could stay under pressure. Maybe if I could walk through Maria's inferno with my emotions on a tight rein there'd be no need to worry about my mental state when I met Herrera. If I could go through this, maybe I could go through anything.

I piled up my excuses one by one, building up to the critical threshold of agreement.

"Okay," I said, finally—and the trudging seconds of the pause must have added up to a nice stack of credit notes at the rates she was charging for her services. "Show me the script."

She showed me the script, and ran bits of it on the holo unit which turned her desk top into a crystal ball.

It started out with about fifteen minutes SD. That isn't enough to reduce anyone to a gibbering wreck although some people with preconceived ideas about what should happen do manage to tear themselves apart in much shorter times. So far as I was concerned it would just hypersensitize my brain.

The fear run came next. Instead of the solid models that the standard tests use she had devised vague, half-formed images that could only be suggestive in the brief times they were flashed—this was a kind of 3-D Rorschach test, reaching at my subconscious through the interpretative prejudices of my visual habits. Standard fear-reaction tests are clumsy but quantifiable—this one was sophisticated but quite unquantitative. She reckoned that didn't matter.

After this run there was a rest phase, then more SD. She explained that situation testing had been left out entirely as I'd be incapable of identifying with most sim situations as if they were real. The exception was the ring, but she'd already observed me in the ring quite exhaustively. What she'd done instead was to put together fragments of nonsensical events— bits of dreams. Dream landscapes and dream events. These were supposed to exploit the mind-opening potential of the superficially absurd. When meaning is unclear, the mind gropes for it. The subconscious will try to find meanings to fit, and will compare them against the dream sequence, hoping to impose a pattern of common sense. The incomprehensible, she thought, was bound to engage my mind and make it work—even if I was only conscious of the activity as a kind of puzzle-solving.

I looked at some of the sequences, and they seemed innocuous enough—crazy collages of ideas like surrealistic paintings.

Finally, I confirmed my agreement and we set a time for the test—in the evening, after the day's work-out. It would have to be late because the machine would have to be prepared and I would need time to recover from a long afternoon in the hot seat.

The first period of sensory deprivation was the worst part of the whole performance. SD is one of those things which works all the better when you put up more psychological resistance. Some people under SD are hysterical in a matter of minutes because they know that's what's supposed to happen and they talk themselves into it. People who fight like hell to stay calm and unbothered go hysterical in pretty much the same way—exhausting themselves in a battle that needn't be fought. It's like the old joke about winning a prize if you can spend five minutes thinking about a horse but not about its tail.

SD is not something you can get used to. Your brain remains awake and alert, but cut off from all sensory input it reacts by stages, with no reference at all to consciousness. The first thing it does is to "turn up the volume" on all the input devices which ought to be bringing in information but aren't—that is to say, it becomes responsive to stimuli which would normally be well below the awareness threshold, like the movement of the blood in the veins and the feel of internal muscular contractions.

Unless you have a particularly creaky body, though, that isn't enough to satisfy the brain's processing faculties. Then, one of two things can happen. Either the brain can begin to switch off its processing faculties (but without switching off or turning down its input receptors) or it can begin to process "secondary information"—information recovered from the memory tapes. In the first instance the subject goes into a quasi-hypnotic trance. In the second, he begins to dream or hallucinate. In either case, though, he is still awake and alert—the *pons* is not activated so as to switch off the body-machine and let the mind lapse into sleep.

A long session of SD can make the brain do peculiar things, and breaking into a long-established sequence of SD with external stimuli can cause severe disturbance. But ten or twenty minutes—provided that the subject is neither over-reactive nor over-resistant—merely serves to make the mind more receptive to stimuli, which will seem exaggerated and call forth exaggerated emotional responses. Very helpful to a PT who is vamping the subject's mind.

When the patterns began to come at me my mind was taken by storm. I was more or less helpless to put conscious shackles on my subconscious—and thus supposedly natural—reactivity.

The images were in color, but the color was just glamour, misleading my practiced eye and undermining my ability to identify shapes on the spur of the moment. It was the shapes that were important and it was the shapes that my mind would use as signs in order to design responses. Aversion reactions would go out across the B-link clear as a bell, though I'd probably not feel anything much myself—E-resonance works off physiological changes of state connected with emotion, not the way that emotions are actually experienced—after subconscious censorship—in the mind.

I could feel myself reacting, not with the kind of fear which comes to you when you see something about to hurt you, but with the kind of vague, unreasoning disturbance which sometimes assaults you in dreams—itself rather fearful because you can't identify its source.

I knew that somewhere out in the streaming shadows were all the things on the list of common and neurotic phobic responses—spiders and wasps, shadows and pet dogs, crowds and midgets, confined spaces and vast vistas of emptiness, long drops and sheer walls. But they all went by too fast for any kind of *considered* reaction.

I tried, reflexively, to recoil from it all—to withdraw, the way you sometimes try desperately to wake up from a dream which has become too nasty to stay in. But you can't wake up when you aren't asleep. And you can't shut your eyes when the visual images are being pumped through silver wires straight into your inner being.

Strangely, I got a sudden burst of curiosity. I wondered what all this would look like from an objective viewpoint—from Maria Kenrian's shoes. I tried to estimate how much of what might be getting through.

Somewhere, I told myself, my secret fear is being reflected in the jigging of a mechanical lever—pointed out by a needle swinging across the face of a dial. I'm being read, like one of those frustrated virgin books in the library—my calf covers tipped aside to make the pages yield up their meaning, display it to the naked eye.

Some people, I know, find themselves enmeshed by terror in dreams where they experience a sudden loss of support. Others find the ultimate self-test in sensations of utter immobility, where they find themselves desperate to run while their bodies are too heavy to allow them to lift a limb.

But I felt no terror, no desperation. What happened, happened—all that resounded in me was a casual nausea—a gut-twisting that threatened to knot my being. There was no semblance of retreat or of mental collapse.

But I felt lonely.

When it was over, and my sim body was sitting in a sim chair in a sim room, waiting for phase two to begin, I was struck by the thought of how absurd it is that we know ourselves so very slightly.

As the music soothed me, I almost laughed at the trivial cosmic joke which makes us need psychotherapists. How is it that we must be so unfamiliar with our own minds? How is it that we need ingenious tests of subtlety and sophistication in order to decoy the consciousness away so that outsiders can get a peep at what we really are?

Why *aren't* we aware of the roots of our fears, the bases of our hopes, the fundamentals of our ambitions? Isn't it ridiculous that *others* should see us as we need to see ourselves, while for the most part we cannot?

Sometimes, I think the only explanation for human existence is that God must be a committee.

Suddenly, in the room with the piped music, an image appeared. It was Dr. Kenrian, complete with white coat and synthetic smile. A nice touch.

"All set?" she asked.

I didn't respond, not by so much as a twitch of the face. I wasn't programmed for it.

"Phase two begins now," she said.

Then it all went dark again. The silence rang in my ears. The sense of touch fell away from me, leaving me enfolded by nonexistence.

The vague feeling of disturbance, of existential dislocation, was still lurking in the canyons of my mind like one of those black dogs people used to talk about. I let it lurk, and tried to remain easy and comfortable while the SD magnified my mind for the second time.

Then the fragments began to feed in.

Again the rate of flow seemed fast—up-tempo of normal experience—but this time the abstraction of shapes which had initially served to conceal the visual cues from conscious-ness was replaced by the juxtaposition of absurd assemblies of coalesced images. The whole images usually included action—events as well as images—and seemed to last some time longer than the thirty seconds or so they actually did. They ran into one another, making a sequence which seemed totally fantastic—unreal or surreal. Consciously I could identify and make sense out of the parts of each vision, but when it came to integrating the whole into a "situation" my conscious mind was left flat-footed. Only the subconscious, with a vocabulary of symbols far more versatile—if less rich—than that available to the rational mind, had any chance to make something of them.

As is the case with dreams, very few of the elements of the

sequence made more than the most transient impression on the surface of the memory.

There was a street, outside a room whose perspective misled the eye. A bulbous lamp, lighting the room from without, an external stair winding down the outer wall from above. Cobwebs over a bed—slept in but no longer occupied, possibly left untended for years. A feeling of dryness. Movement slow, invisible. Light creeping in through corners—

running into—

An eye. Reflections in the eye of standing screens, like Venetian blinds, mounted on curved legs. Between the screens, sand, wind-drifted. Clouds above. At the back of the image, behind all other reflected objects, the reflection of an eye, staring into the eye which holds it. And in the eye, screens—

And so, ad infinitum—

An eagle in a blue-violet sky, storm clouds and silence. Heavy air. Underneath, poplars in a long line. An alleyway with stones glistening, not with rain. Figures moving—a girl, gray-white and unreal, perhaps a statue—is raped. The rapists move in jerks, like puppets. She is forced to the ground, then folded. One of the men has sandals, their eyes are all concealed. An abundance of red in the image, but it will not settle on any object or field of vision. It escapes any direct association—

but flees—

Cold fire in the air, or perhaps we are under the sea. The world swirls, and sparkles. Figures entwine. It is impossible to identify the arms with the legs, to separate the limbs into sets, into identities. There is simply a liquid mass of humanity, a coenocyte. There may be volcanoes in the distance, there may be fish skimming the surface of the sand. There are plants—dendritic weeds—etched in shadow—

which falls—

Bulbous leaves. A rich, all-engulfing foliage. In the branches, movement. In the stillness, an owl, with entrails hanging from its mouth—the torn body of mouse or shrew. In the grass, movement, but sitting still, with infinite patience in its eye, a leopard.

Alive, but motionless. Hungry. Alert.

Blink—

Cobbled streets. Downhill, a river. Many bridges, so that the river flows mostly under concrete, exposed to the air in bare patches. Its waters rank. In the streets, soldiers. Other people walk too quickly, everyone in a hurry. A double-decker bus carries us among them. We are the enemy, but undetected. At any moment, there may be fighting or an escape. The bus moves too slowly. The street gets steeper. The waters are black—

swirling and swelling—

And more.

I search for faceless men, soft clocks, snakes, guns. I look for staircases enclosed by tight walls, battlements and bandages. There are none of these. The symbols are always elusive—when the mind begins to decode, the code is changed. The symbols shift and obliquity retains its supremacy. One part of the mind enquires, another conjures.

I feel sweat on my face, and realize that reality is seeping back into the dream. The tech is dismantling the apparatus. Maria is standing by, having already discarded the B-link by which she has been a spectator in my mind.

Blink—

I felt curiously naked. I never like coming out of a sim if there are people around who have been riding my mind, but this was even worse. After being in the ring, I know exactly what has happened. I know what the vamps have been sucking. But this time I had just been a piece of window-glass.

I felt very tired.

I wanted to ask questions, but I didn't want to hear the answers.

"Well?" I said, harshly.

She smiled faintly. "Take it easy," she advised.

"Sure."

When the last of the electrodes was tucked away, and the caps replaced, I got up and flexed my arms.

"You seem to be okay," I told her. "How am I?"

"Balanced," she said.

"As sane as you are?"

She shrugged. "Tomorrow," she said. "I'll come out here again. We'll talk about it then. Not now."

I was half-glad of the way out—but only half-glad. I went back to the house and to bed. Where I thought for a while—and then dreamed.

I can't remember where I went in my dreams, but I know that when I woke next morning I was in a better frame of mind. I was not simply ready, but anxious, to get answers to the questions—to find out how the enemy's plan of campaign was coming along.

I had to wait, of course—all day. But the routine was just routine and it was easy enough to cruise through by now. I finally got to see her after the evening meal, in one of the multiplicity of small rooms with neither name nor function which seemed to proliferate endlessly throughout Valerian's great house. She seemed well-satisfied and confident, but it might just have been the face she wore for such occasions as this one.

"Well," I said, in my customary opening tone of jovial hostility, "have you catalogued the contents of my soul?"

"More or less," she replied.

"And what are my secret fears?"

"Nothing so very unusual. Or particularly secret. Like most of us, you fear death and other people, not necessarily in that order."

I couldn't tell whether this was an answer or whether it was a subtle brand of repartee. I didn't say anything. She leaned forward slightly in her chair.

"There's only one way that you're going to win this fight— the fight against Herrera," she said.

I waited.

"You have to overcome your present ambiguity of attitude. You can't go into the ring with your resentment of Valerian getting in the way. You want Herrera to lose, and you want Valerian to lose, and there's a conflict of interests. That conflict has to be resolved."

"You want me to learn to love Valerian?" I said. It was something I'd always suspected.

"That wouldn't work," she said. "What can be done, though, is to make you desire to see Herrera beaten stronger than your desire to cross Valerian."

"There's nothing stronger than my desire to beat Herrera," I said.

"That's not quite what I said," she pointed out. "You want to win—but winning isn't such a simple thing. In your present state of mind you could get slaughtered in the ring and come out believing—honestly and sincerely—that you'd won, that you'd beaten Valerian out of his revenge. That's the danger of the mixed motives, you see—they offer you an excuse. I want to sharpen your personal animosity against Herrera. You don't like him, or what he stands for—but you don't quite hate him, not the way you hate Velasco Valerian.

"What I went looking for in your mind is a way to sharpen you against Herrera, a way to make him into an image to be destroyed."

"In other words," I said, quietly, "to make me feel about him the way Valerian feels."

"Yes."

I stood up and went to the window, not because I wanted to look out but because I wanted to get away from her for a few minutes.

"And you think you can do it?" I asked.

"Yes."

Outside, there were starlings on the grass, pecking at something. I couldn't imagine what. Everyone knows that it's only early birds who get worms.

"Seen your way," I said, "this is a thoroughly dirty business, isn't it? We have nothing in which to trade but hatreds and fears. Suffering and anguish. That's what makes your world turn around. That's what people are made of, according to your recipe. Not even frogs and snails and what the hell. Just neuroses, just tastefully draped vices. You want me to win, and in your book that's synonymous with wanting me to hate. You see no more in it than that. You live in a cruel world."

I turned back to look at her. She was perfectly relaxed in a chair that seemed a couple of sizes too big for her. Her silver hair was neat and slick, as if sprayed with molten metal. Her slender features were made-up, the flaws in her skin—the moles, the pores, the thin lines—all covered over. Packaged. And behind the mask? When she took off her face, was there a snake-locked gorgon waiting within? For all I knew, she might cry vitriol tears.

"My methods work," she said.

"They shouldn't," I told her.

"Your cynicism slipped then," she said, calmly. "Just for a moment."

I couldn't think of anything to do with my hands, and all of a sudden I thought they seemed spare, ugly. I put them in my pockets.

"I had this dream," I said to her, keeping a perfectly straight face, though she couldn't see it. "I was swimming in the Arctic Sea. I was just on the point of freezing to death when I was swallowed by a giant flatfish. It was the same one that got Jonah—never mind that crap about whales, it was a giant flatfish. Inside, it was pretty dark, so I struck a match and found myself alone with this transparent girl. I held the match a little closer to get a better look at her, never having seen a transparent girl before, and she recoiled from its heat. I saw the surface of her arm begin to melt, and I realized that she was a water nymph who'd somehow frozen over.

"And that, you see, was my introduction to one of the great enigmas of life. Right there and then, the question popped into my mind, and I said, 'What's an ice girl like you doing in a plaice like this?'"

Surprisingly, she laughed.

"Someone," I said, "should found a new school of psychotherapy based on the analysis of the jokes their patients tell.

Even if no one got any saner everybody concerned could have a damn good laugh. As a method, it's just mad enough to catch on. Nobody ever lost money by inviting the public to make fools of themselves and demanding a fee for the privilege."

There was a brief silence.

"And?" she prompted.

"And what?"

"And now you've steered well away from the point at issue. Now what?"

I turned back to the window. "You can forget the point at issue," I said. "I'll do my own fighting. I won't be programmed like a guard dog to go for the throat as soon as I see the bogey man."

"What about the tests?"

"What about them?"

"Don't you want to know what they indicate? Don't you want to know *how* you can learn to hate Herrera?"

"No," I said. "I'd rather not. Lead us not into temptation. I think the matter is better left where it belongs—inside my head. I'll work out my own way to beat Herrera. In a boxing match— not a war of extermination. It's not a matter of life and death."

"Maybe not death," she said, demurely, "but life—"

She got up and went to the door.

"You can always phone me," she said, as she left. "Any time between now and the big night."

CHAPTER ELEVEN

I won the preliminary fight, and I won it very much my way. Skillful, efficient, easy in my mind.

It pulled an audience of nearly a million and the sixty percent who tied into me saw an exhibition of boxing that might even have come close to teaching them what it was all about. A lot of them, though, were probably bored stiff, cruising on whatever enthusiasm their own humble, tired brains could work up. But you get no guarantees when you set off on a free ride. They'd just have to put up with it.

Afterwards, there were a few reporters to be seen, and a tiny knot of fight fans who'd fluttered in from the environs in heli-cabs as soon as the fight was over, in the hope of finding an argument or a good screw, depending on sex (theirs, not mine). It never ceases to amaze me how it doesn't click with some suckers that the guy who's handling a sim is not necessarily gifted by nature with the same six-three Apollonic persona as the image in the holo set. There must be thousands of ex-teen-agers whose dreams of super-orgasm were smashed forever the first time they set eyes on the *real* Paul Herrera.

Out of the crowd I picked the one man who interested me, and invited him to join our party for a drink. I was entitled to a mild celebration, though Wolff came along to make sure I didn't do anything which might faintly prejudice my peak condition. The fact that I leave my body behind when I go into the ring didn't mean that I could have *carte blanche* to mistreat it—not as far as Wolff was concerned. He believed that a *mens sana* needs a *corpore sano*, and he had jurisdiction over that particular aspect of my life. To get anywhere at all in this world you have to give bits of yourself away—surrender your sacred choices two by two.

Only four of us wound up sitting round the table in the club, however. Valerian declined to accompany us. Of the four, only one was drinking as if he meant it, and he seemed to mean it very hard indeed. Wolff, Angeli and myself practiced moderation, but such considerations as we had in mind obviously didn't bother our companion, Mr. Sacchetti.

The cabaret was awful, and I wondered how come the entertainment business was supposed to be thriving. But I hadn't really come to watch bouncing breasts and listen to sculptures in sound.

"Did you enjoy the fight?" I asked the reporter.

"Sure," he said. "I enjoy all fights. Some people are hard to please, but I'm easy."

"Your comrades-in-arms are going to slay me again," I said. "They still think I fight too fair. How about you?"

He shrugged. "We'll all be in the middle ground tomorrow," he said. "They'll have advanced, I'll have retreated. The controversy has to die. No more point in it."

He wasn't saying anything particularly bitter, but I could feel a real hardness in the way he spoke. Most people, when they take a lot of liquor, get softer in the voice, begin to slacken. But this guy just turned to stone. He could say, "I love you" like he was spitting powdered glass. I realized that he hated the fight game. That was why he wrote about it. In his reports, I'd looked for a kindred spirit, and hadn't found one. Even so, I'd been reluctant to believe that Valerian was right and that he was just a damn-it-all committed cynic. I'd hoped to find him able to believe in the same things I did. Skill and sport. But he didn't. He was a skeptic through and through.

"It was a good, clean fight," I told him. "Nothing for the vamps. That's the way it should be."

"It was a straight kill," he said, neutrally. "You want a medal?"

"Why not?"

He looked at me in a peculiar way. His face was pointing somewhere else, but his eyes were on mine. "You think you're something special?" he asked.

"Don't you?"

"You're okay," he said, rather grudgingly. "You maybe have a heart of gold. You don't do much for the hungry fans. Yet. But if you think you can beat the system you're a mug. *It* will beat *you*. It already is."

"I don't get you," I said.

He glanced down at his drink, checking to see if there were enough dregs to make it worth the effort of lifting the glass to his lips. There were. He shook his bead as he swallowed. "There's no way out. Okay, so first time out you were a poke in the eye with a sharp stick. They deserved you. But they'll make you over into what they want you to be. You think they're only sitting on your skull, picking up the crumbs you care to drop, but it's not that simple. They suck you up, they weaken you, they stir around in your head, and in the end you give them what they need. Vultures don't just wait for things to die, you know—they give a helping hand now and again, like a peck or a slash with their claws. You can't keep cold with a hundred million hungry worms in your skull. It isn't possible. Tonight, six hundred thousand—tomorrow, the whole world. Even tonight, you were yielding, just a fraction. When you take on Herrera you can't resist. If you beat him, you'll become him. That's the way it goes. The vamps make their victims." He ran a rigid finger across his throat, and looked at me as if the vultures were sitting all around me, waiting to begin.

I'd heard it all before, of course. Even from Stella.

Ray Angeli objected violently to Sacchetti's line of argument, though I wasn't quite sure why. He strung together some semi-articulate challenge. I didn't listen to the words—I already knew the tune too well.

Sacchetti was cruel to the kid. I guess he was cruel to everybody. He didn't even look as if he liked his mother. "You lost, son," he said. "You weren't good enough. You don't know what the score is any more than your friend does. But I've seen it. I've been around a long time. I know you, and I know how you'll be in five years and ten, and right up to the day they've sucked you dry of fight and feeling. Even Herrera was a man once, but now he's what they made him—a flash storm. Everything he ever was only exists when he's in the ring, to be yanked out by the vamps. Have you seen Herrera in the flesh recently? Have *you?*" This last was addressed to me.

I hadn't seen Paul Herrera in the flesh. Not for more years than I cared to remember. In my mind's eye, he was still a kid—a Burne Caine.

"He's just a dance," said Sacchetti. "A dance to the music of the mind-riders."

"That's pretty," I said. "Pure journalese, subspecies inside back page. But you're missing out. You're painting it all black, and it isn't."

"Every silver lining is locked inside a cloud," he said, and laughed politely at himself. It wasn't funny.

There was no point in insisting. I was disappointed by Sacchetti. It seemed that everywhere I looked for the least vestige of moral support there was nothing but black humor or an intellectual vacuum. Even Wolff couldn't really be on my side, because in his eyes only half the problem existed. To him, there were no vamps. They didn't exist. Wolff's idea of the universe didn't extend outside the ropes of the ring. I bet he didn't believe in atoms, either.

I begrudged paying for Sacchetti's liquor. He was as much use to me as a pet mockingbird.

I withdrew into my thoughts as Ray Angeli began to tell me again how to beat Herrera. I withdrew, but I couldn't switch off my eyes. They kept roaming around, showing me bleak faces and colored light and actors on a stage paid to make fools of themselves for the delectation of the public. But there were no vamps here. All the applause was polite, and anyone who got high did so on innocent chemical compounds.

I was assaulted by the thought that nobody in the world wanted me to win the title fight—not my way. Some other way, maybe. But nobody wanted to come over to my side of the fence, to look at it from my angle. They all wanted to stay up on their own safe pedestals. I wished I could topple the lot—Valerian, Stella, Wolff, Angeli, Sacchetti, Maria—tumble them into doubt, make them all re-think themselves out of utter confusion.

But there's no way you can do that. Those pedestals are built to last.

In the papers next day there were rumors.

Above, below and beside reports on my fight and my title hopes there were carefully-constructed whispers about Paul Herrera. He was ill, scared, mad, old, disappointed in love. Nobody actually said so, but they sowed the seeds. It was the idlest of idle speculation, but that's how the so-called news is made. It was all due to Valerian. He was cleaning the dead bodies out of the arena, putting down new sawdust to cover the old blood. The lions were back in their cages, the disemboweled Christians in Heaven, and the gladiators were sleeping with their swords. Somebody had to go out and make the masses believe that tomorrow it was all going to be new, unexpected, exciting. Not just the same old circus served with yesterday's stale bread.

You have to admire the technique. The sun never sets on Network's Empire, and they worked hard to ensure that it was never likely to.

I felt blurred, as if I didn't quite have myself in focus. In the morning session I chased Angeli round the ring for a desultory couple of rounds, and never really looked like catching him. Farcically, in the third I saw him slowing down, deliberately miscuing his gentle jabs. He wanted me to hit him, to be fast and good. He wasn't really handling his own sim at all. He wanted to identify with me. He wanted me to be superman, to beat Herrera, to do what he wanted to do but hadn't.

I knocked him down a couple of times, rousing myself slightly from my torpor. I hit him rather harder than was warranted, and after I'd thus shown off my contempt I felt rather guilty—not because I'd hurt him but because I'd somehow betrayed myself. I'd let myself be decoyed into the game, letting frustration put power in my punches.

I found it difficult to recover real poise and efficiency. Wolff bitched at me and I bitched back.

By the end of the afternoon I was feeling even lower—very much at odds with the world and with myself. It was only a mood, and it would pass, but it was a bad thing to be stuck in. The day seemed to drag, and it seemed peculiarly devoid of presence and incident. Valerian was away, and there were just two of us at dinner—myself and Curman. I asked him why he wasn't with the old man and he explained that he had to go out later with Stella. After this exchange of information I let the conversation go to hell, and applied myself with fiendish concentration to the food which still, to me, tasted alien and unpleasant. After I finished eating, though, I began to slow down, deliberately taking it easy over the coffee, letting time go by and not making any effort to carry myself through into a new phase of existence.

Curman was waiting, too—waiting, I supposed, for the mercurial Stella to show up and demand his company. We must have looked as if we were doing some really serious research into techniques for wasting time.

"Not so good," he commented, eventually, as if in answer to an imaginary question. He apparently thought that it was time for a second attempt at conversation.

The silence didn't want to yield, but we forced it into submission.

"On the contrary," I said. "It's heaven when the roses are in bloom."

"All roses got thorns," he quoted, dolefully. It was about the level of wit one would expect from a character like Curman.

"Have a drink, why don't you?" I said, nodding toward the cabinet at the side. "Or do they put wax crayon marks on the bottles."

He shook his head, and made no move. He was inventing some new remark, which would probably be as facile as all the rest, when he was interrupted by Stella's entry into the room.

She sailed in confidently and sat down. With near-miraculous precision the first course materialized in front of her. I watched the waiter disappear, and wondered how he did it.

"How's things?" I asked, politely.

"Same as always," she replied, and added—with a glance at Curman—"pretty deadly."

"Why?" I inquired.

She seemed surprised by the question. She didn't answer it.

"Unrequited love?" I prompted. "Or did you lose a bet?"

"Both," she replied. She didn't seem interested in gay repartee. "Better get the car out," she said to Curman. He nodded and sauntered out.

"Alone at last," I said.

"If your punches are as lousy and predictable as your dialogue," she said, "you'll get all hell knocked out of you when you go up against Herrera."

"He'll have to catch me first. Where are you going?"

"To the dogs," she said.

I must have looked startled.

"They race, you know," she added, by way of explanation. "It's a sport."

"Oh," I said. "You mean literally to the dogs."

"I own some," she said. "Cheaper than horses. It's one of my private vices—one of the few I'm allowed. The old man owns boxers, I own greyhounds. His are losers, mine sometimes win. Sporting blood runs in the family, like old books. All the way back to our remotest ancestors, in the nineteen twenties."

"That's not so far."

"True," she admitted. "Some of my dogs have longer pedigrees than I have. But I can always borrow some of their respectability. Or marry into a family that can trace itself back to Genghis Khan."

I couldn't think of a witty reply.

"You want some advice," she said. She had somehow picked up Curman's habit of saying things like that without the question mark that other people reckon to be polite.

"A hot tip?" I asked.

"That's right," she said. "Get out now. Don't let that bitch screw your mind. She's got something in the works. She told granddaddy that you wouldn't play and they've decided to stop giving you the option. Tomorrow, they'll cut your heart out. Or maybe the next day."

I pretended not to take it seriously for all of thirty seconds. But I couldn't think of a way to dodge the issue. It wasn't one of my creative days. Finally, I said, "How do you know?"

"I know," she said, in the tone of one who did. "And I know she's a bitch. I know one when I see one. I've got two chasing a hare for me tonight. They're stupid, because they don't know the hare's electric. Don't let them hustle you. It can't be worth it."

I was surprised by the venom in her voice when she talked about bitches. I conjured up a lightning fantasy about Maria seducing Valerian, marrying him and inheriting everything, leaving Stella to play Cinderella. It didn't seem very likely.

The waiter appeared with the main course.

"Forget it," she said. "I'll get a sandwich."

Just like that, she was gone.

"Fooled you," I commented, as the poor guy looked down at his lovely food, and then round at the uncaring walls and the open door.

I sat there for long minutes, toying with the cannonade of phrases Stella had fired before leaving. If she was right, the barriers were down. Valerian wanted action from his pet boxer and action he was going to have. A dirty game.

But what was there to do? Running was out of the question. Whatever they had planned for me I'd have to take. And resist. I'd spurned the velvet glove and the chance to cooperate with a smile. Now I'd have to grit my teeth. There was no possible escape.

Sometimes, you just have to be a hero and let the bastards come at you.

CHAPTER TWELVE

Despite what the proverbial wisdom of the masses has to say, forewarned is not necessarily forearmed. I sallied forth next morning expecting to face the torturers of the Inquisition, but in no way prepared or ready for them.

The techs strapped me into the apparatus just the same way as ever, and there was no sign of anything out of place, but I could feel that something was amiss. I was looking over my shoulder until the last possible moment, trying to spot Dr. Kenrian making one of her famous unobtrusive entrances.

But it wasn't until they were about to clamp the mask in place, when I was immobile and totally helpless, that the trap finally clicked and I was in it. It wasn't the doctor, but Valerian. I think he enjoyed it.

They were putting the mask on, so that I couldn't see him. His voice was tinny and muffled.

"We're going to try something new this morning," he said.

With my jaw tied, I couldn't say a word—and that was a cruel twist, because there was some real poison I wanted to pour out. I couldn't stop him, but I could sure as hell let him know what I thought about it. He wouldn't have minded listening—he was honest enough to let you say things to his face—but he wanted the operation to go smoothly, without any interruption.

"We had a conference last night," he said. "By 'we' I mean Mr. Wolff, Dr. Kenrian and myself. We thought that it was time your training became a little more *specific*—directed toward the particular goal that we all share. What we intend to do is to allow you to get a long, hard look at Paul Herrera—his style, his strength. It's important that you should know your enemy, and know everything about him. That's an advantage he won't have, because you've not yet been extended to your limit in the ring. He has, or very nearly so.

"What will happen now—and on a number of mornings yet to come—is that we'll implant your viewpoint in the sim of the challenger during recorded playback of a number of Herrera's fights. Not too many, because we don't want to get you into the habit of being knocked out by Herrera. From your viewpoint you'll have the perfect opportunity to study Herrera, in all respects. We want you to undertake this coolly and calmly—stay detached as far as possible. This is perhaps the most important element in your entire training program."

And there, his voice still oozing malicious irony, he let it lie.

I knew there was a catch, and he knew I knew. He had hinted at the fact in his tone. Yet on the surface, it seemed reasonable. Get a good long look at Herrera in the ring. Study him. Coolly and calmly—as an academic exercise. Wolff had helped draw up this plan, so it seemed like a good idea to him too. So where was the barb?

And then I was in the ring. I consoled myself with the thought that here, at least, even the Inquisition had to fight by the rules.

While the body I was riding was still in the corner I could feel that it was for real. You can be a passenger in a handled sim and know that it's fake, staged or programmed. The whole way the body is held by its handler testifies to the priorities in operation. This body was tense, active in a thousand small ways, ready to go.

I felt the sim moving, walking into the center of the ring. The other fighter came to meet me. I was riding the black, and for a moment that didn't click. I knew who the white sim was but I looked into the features, searching for recognition-signs, and wondering why it was so strange, so unfamiliar. It was the standard blank face, not yet tightened up by its wearer into a recognizable expression.

The gloves touched, and we were moving in earnest.

I was caught up, for a few seconds, by the sensation of being in a wholly alien situation. It was so familiar and yet so different. I was just a passenger, riding the body of another fighter, a man who had fought Herrera—and failed.

—and *failed.*

Then it struck me. Herrera was wearing the white. But Herrera was the champion. Herrera wore black. Always. Except—

I knew then that I was trapped in the body of Franco Valerian. This body had taken a pounding worse than any other in the short history of this wonderful sport. And the man who had handled it had died of the experience. Franco, of course, had gone through the fight in a state of blissful innocence. He hadn't known what was happening. But I did.

And this was Maria's way to my innermost heart. I realized then how exquisitely mixed were the motives that had led the three conspirators to set this thing up. Wolff wanted me to learn to fight Herrera, Maria wanted me to learn to hate him, and Valerian—Valerian wanted me in Franco's place, the place I should have been, the place where Franco died instead of me.

It all tied up.

And the tests—the tests Maria had conducted. They had confirmed what she already knew, and what I *ought* to have known. They had confirmed my weak point—a horror of violence. Not fear—I wasn't *afraid* of being hurt—but horror. Something like disgust. The disgust which had stopped me and let Burne Caine knock me down. The disgust that made me fight the way I did. The disgust that I felt for the vamps, who fed on violence, and for Herrera, who manufactured it for them.

I thought, for one brief moment, of one of the images that I recalled from the artificial dream sequence she had fed to me—one significant moment out of many. There had been a scene where I was witness to a rape, and I had seen the victim of that rape as a *statue,* something unreal, something that was *folded up* and put away afterwards. I knew, suddenly, that that was only the way my mind had chosen to interpret it. The rape had been real, but I had masked it, seen it another way. A horror of violence.

I realized then, perhaps for the first time in my life, the foundation stone upon which my life as a fighter had been built. We all sail close to our everyday fears, steering a course that will help us avoid them while seeming to overcome them. I knew, in that moment, what my need to win really was.

And thus Maria Kenrian's work was done. All in a flash. Everything she wanted to tell me, wanted to force me to know. It was all there. And now I had to live in it, and in Franco Valerian, while Herrera destroyed us.

I was floating round the ring, being carried round by Franco's head. The body was probing, parrying, dodging. I could almost relax, be carried along, paying no real attention to it all. As if it was a dream. But I knew that pain, if nothing else, was going to break through the euphoria and confirm the reality of it all. If it was a dream, it was a dream from which I could not wake up.

I watched the white sim.

I saw Herrera.

I looked at what the white was doing, and how. I could see in its style, its tempo, its character, something I knew very well, something that reached out through all the years—a great continuity of familiarity. I'd watched Herrera in the ring so many times, and faced him there once. Through all that, there had been aspects of his action that marked him—aspects of his identity that time and skill and experience had not changed.

In the first two rounds, it was just an ordinary fight. It lacked finesse, it lacked a thousand little things that no one had mastered in those distant days. From the point of view of an old-style boxing purist it was a lousy fight, one cut above a brawl. After the second, maybe even being one cut above was a compliment. It became a brawl—and it stopped being ordinary.

In the third, Herrera came forward and forward and forward. He put solid blows into the body of the sim I was riding, shaking it, weakening it, hurting it. This was far more the Herrera I'd fought and beaten than the Herrera Angeli had fought and lost, but one *vital* change had occurred. Something inside him, invisible to the eye, had turned him into a winner.

My mind strayed back, searching for the memory of this fight, trying to remember exactly the way it had gone. It should have been engraved on me forever, but all I could remember was that Herrera had started hammering and had gone on hammering. In the fourth and the fifth and the sixth. And on, and on. The only thing I could remember was the wonderment I'd experienced when I couldn't understand what unearthly power kept bringing Franco back for more.

Franco had put up the most astonishing display of blind, stupid courage ever seen in Technicolor. An exhibition in taking punishment. An exhibition, as it was ultimately to prove, in sticking it out to the bitterest end of them all.

And why?

In my mind, I could only plot the pattern of the event. I couldn't separate causes from effects. Sometimes you can't.

Paul Herrera had come out of a childhood and adolescence of poverty and unbearable misery. To say he had a grudge against the world would be an understatement. He needed so desperately to win because he knew so acutely everything there is to know about losing. He was flat out to take every advantage of the situation which allowed him, temporarily, to be on the same terms—absolutely equal terms—with *the enemy.* Nothing personal—it wasn't that Franco was a rich man's son. To Paul Herrera, life itself was *the enemy.* He didn't blame the system, because he didn't know any alternatives.

And Franco? Franco knew nothing. There was nothing in his background that could have taught him. He was the son of Velasco Valerian, last of the feudal overlords, heir to a heritage of decay that was no less ridiculous because it was all fake, pretense and imitation, dating all the way back to 1920. Franco had never lost in his life, never known the meaning of the word. He had never been on equal terms with anything in the world before, and he didn't know what an enemy was.

Winning and losing, like loving and hating, are not things

which happen to you. They're things you have to learn to do.

Franco wouldn't have had the sense to come in out of the rain. He'd have asked for the sky to be switched off. He didn't have the sense to lie down when Herrera kept hitting him—he just kept getting up and trying to switch the sky off. He'd expected a miracle. It was his birthright.

Only those rules don't hold in the ring. Whom the gods of wealth destroy, they first make poor. Poor Franco. In the currency of the ring, he was a bankrupt.

And I was locked inside his body, getting beaten up along with him. Supposedly learning to hate. I felt the gloves finding my flesh time and time again, marking the sim body, marking Franco's mind. This was Valerian's justice. I was supposed to be suffering.

But I wasn't. Not his way. I was hurting, but I didn't mind the pain. I'm not afraid of being hurt—I've been hurt too often for that. The wounds which had killed Franco were psychological, not physical, and I wasn't feeling those. I was just getting hit. But as an actor, handling villains, I'd been hit and killed—in simulation—a hundred times and more. It didn't bother me. The things I'd handled had been shot, impaled, burned to death, and as often as not I'd been in there to the bitter end giving the last few twitches to make it all look as corny as hell.

Sims in melodramas feel no pain, but it wasn't the pain that had killed Franco. It had been commitment and involvement to a false notion of the way the world worked. I didn't have that, and not even Velasco Valerian's sleight of mind could give it to me. Phase one of his revenge was a bust.

The fight went on, through the sixth and the seventh.

The seventh, I knew, had been the real crisis point. At the end of the seventh Franco's sim was virtually staggering as it was driven back to its corner. I could feel the dull, sullen hurt virtually consuming the swollen, pulpy flesh. It all seemed quite meaningless, quite irrelevant. From now on, it seemed to me, Franco could feel no more in his body. From now on it was just a farce—from my lonely, unfeeling viewpoint, that is.

As the sponge danced I was just waiting, waiting for it all to end, and thinking vaguely that I was somehow winning, that they hadn't got me yet.

And I felt a stir of apprehension, as I realized that it was too easy. My mind dredged up a fleeting, faded half-memory that I'd retained through nearly twenty years—from *my* fight against Herrera. It was a kind of internal snapshot, which I'd saved up in the album of my life. It was the image of Herrera's face, seen in close-up as he came out for one of the later rounds. He'd come out like some howling, berserk savage. The image showed a face that was twisted into a shape like no other—like nothing the handsome, neutral features of the sim should have been able to assume. Somehow, then, Herrera had torn aside the cosmetic curtain that was the sum face and let something of his own— something demonic—peep through.

I remembered that, over all the years.

And then I saw it again.

The bell had gone, we were up and moving, and there was the face, reproduced as Herrera worked up the same degree of fury. Only this time, the demon was going to have its way.

And that was the moment that Maria chose to produce her extra ace. I thought it was all over, but it was really only just about to begin. The *real* torture—the mindbender.

People talk about floods of emotion, but I don't know what they mean to imply. I don't know the way people live their emotions, and I can't tell whether the words they use to describe such experiences are appropriate. But I'm sure that there is no way they could understand the deluge of feeling which caught me up in that moment.

The people who were E-linked to the fight on that dim and distant day felt what I felt, but they had been built up to it, slowly prepared for it. I was hurled into it, at its deepest point. One moment there was nothing but dull pain, the next the full force of the current whipped me away out of my depth.

A flood of emotion. And I thought I would surely drown.

People commonly believe that in the E-link they are actually experiencing someone else's feelings telepathically, transmitted to them through the machine. But that's not so. What they feel is what they've learned to feel, aroused and stimulated by the resonance-induction mechanism in the headdress. They're stimulated to arouse their *own* feelings.

I wasn't immune, because there's a world of difference between knowing no feelings and keeping them under control. I lost control, under the irresistible pressure of the E-link. The charge pouring into my mind generated wild currents that my mind just had to translate into feelings.

As Paul Herrera's gloves reached the face and body of the black sim again and again and again, I *felt* everything.

I felt savage determination, and the sheer elation of complete superiority. I was high as a kite on adrenalin, cruising the clouds of the mental stratosphere. Seventh heaven. The sensation of winning, exaggerated beyond anything I'd ever felt on my own account.

And the gloves crashed into the sim's jaw, knocking the body sick, grinding the bone, felling the fighter.

I felt the blow burning ecstatically through and through my mind.

They'd crossed the wires. I was in Franco's body, but I was E-linked to Herrera.

I was going to take everything that Herrera would hand out over the next three rounds, get hammered into oblivion. And all the while, I would be feeling what Herrera felt.

Crossed connections, to make a new kind of sense, to spell out a new message, to give me the sharpest lesson of my life, to teach me how to hate.

Maria had set me up two viewpoints for the final rounds of the fight—a crazy kind of binocular vision. I was seeing it all in a totally new perspective, seeing the real four-dimensional depth of what had really happened.

There were just ten more minutes until the end of the fight—ten minutes until Franco went down forever. But those ten minutes I had to spend in mind-split agony. Pain and glory—

the one Franco's, the other Herrera's, but both arising from the same pattern, the pattern of the event. It was only a pattern of light, synthesized by a computer, but its meaning was real and its consequences were real.

I saw both sides of the *charisma* of Paul Herrera, that made him what he was. I saw him as no one—least of all himself— had ever seen him before.

It used to be that you had to die to go through hell, but not in the superscientific age. Not today. They can serve it up off the shelf, just like the heaven you get on prescription. In all versions of hell, from the Inferno on, there has always been some regard for the essential tenet of poetic justice—that punishment should be tailored to fit crime, to provide the horror which the particular subject is least able to bear.

For ten minutes, I was in hell. *My* hell. Paul Herrera was echoing inside me, echoing like something vast and Satanic. I was made to believe that I could feel what Paul Herrera felt, that the human potential in him was in me too. It was the discovery of evil—in him, in me.

And it burned my mind.

CHAPTER THIRTEEN

I came back to life, very slowly. It wasn't really difficult. Franco could have come back too, if he'd only known the way.

With my eyes once again looking out into the real world, and my head throbbing like a great machine as the blood pumped the chemicals of fury away, I was isolated once more.

Maria didn't wait. She began to talk, quickly and quietly.

"It had to be that way," she said. "You had to be made to see. You had to be made to see what it's all about. Now you can win. Now you have the force inside you that will allow you to dedicate yourself *completely* to beating Herrera. This way will work. It has to."

The words just bounced off. Hailstones off a tin drum. A meaningless assault on my sensibilities. I was too sick to stand, too weak to hit out at them, any way at all. And what good would it have done? What was the point? What words could I possibly use to hurt them?

The only way to resist was to take it, to absorb it all. To take it, and remain unchanged. It had to be humanly possible. If I held out against them, they couldn't break my mind. I was only as helpless as I allowed myself to be. I didn't have to react. I could take it all, get up, and walk away, and put it all behind me. What Franco should have done instead of dying.

So I didn't answer back. Not even with clever, sarcastic asides. I just let it all ride on. I let the routine take over, and paid no attention to the vultures. I let Valerian and Maria just fade away, and I didn't care.

The only one I really had to face was Stella. I didn't go to her. She came to me, to say, "I told you so."

And she had. She was entitled.

She found me late in the evening, by the goldfish pond. The setting sun was on my back and I was admiring the total composure of the idle, gawping fish. They just hovered, contemplating the murky infinity beyond their little microcosm. They were perfectly still, as if dreaming.

She came up behind me, and said, "I told you so."

I said, "I know."

"I told you not to do it," she persisted. "Why did you let her?"

"Not just her," I said. "It was a world-wide conspiracy. Fifty million consumers can't be wrong. Not in a democracy."

"You didn't have to take it."

"I want to win."

She must have felt like kicking me, or shoving me into the water.

"Can't you see further than that?" she demanded. "Is that the sum total of what you are—your life, your ambition, your purpose?"

"It doesn't seem such a bad thing to aim at," I said. "Where's your destination in life?"

She didn't answer.

"Did your greyhounds win their races?" I asked, to change the subject.

"The bitch did," she said, her voice pregnant with undeclared sarcasm. "But the dog got kicked to hell and gone on the first bend. These things happen."

"Sure," I said.

"But I don't mind," she went on. "Because it's only a game. It doesn't matter all that much."

"Did the dog know that?" I asked.

"Suppose you *don't* win," she said. It was a point she'd raised before. She was determined to chase it home.

"Then it will all have been for nothing," I told her.

"It's a big gamble," she commented. "You must really trust

your luck."

"There's no such thing," I assured her. I was still looking at the fish. The fish believed me. They knew there was no such thing as luck. Their life was ordained from the word go. No problems.

"Well," she said, slowly, "I guess they haven't exactly changed you into Sir Lancelot. Whatever they did you seem to have lived through it."

"That's the answer," I said. "Live through it. Wait for the time to come. The meek inherit, in the end." I glanced at her then, and I knew she was listening. Maybe I made more sense to her in that moment than ever before—or ever again.

She went away—meekly—to live out her time. And so did I.

The next few weeks were long, but they went by. There were no more dirty tricks where that ace had come from—I played through a few more of Herrera's fights, but I did it the easy way, doing what Wolff thought was proper. Studying the man and his fighting, not the filthy landscapes of his mind. Maria didn't show again, though I knew she'd be back for the kill. Valerian simply continued to be himself, in his own particular way. There was no reference to what had been done by either of us. We just tucked it away in our memories. That part of the game was over. It was a clear run to the next and last. Time dragged while it was going by, but once it had gone it just seemed to disappear. It made no impression on the past, only on the present. Once dead, it just evaporated. I know I lived those weeks and lived them slowly, but in my memory now there's just a hole. From where I stand now in the tangled thread of time, the two events seem almost juxtaposed. Hell—and judgment. Nothing between them but a snatch of conversation with Stella and a vague sense of desolation. They have fled from me like fugitive dreams.

Just like the dream in the sim—

Blink—

As simple as that.

At Network, before the fight, I met Jimmy Schell. He had a new suit and the same stammer. He was making it. It was coming together for him. He was a good feeler, and he was getting good parts to feel. He could feed his riders the kind of charge they needed to wake up what they wanted to feel. That's real talent.

So Network had bought him a new suit. And maybe a new life. And they *loved* his stammer.

"I'll—*be* with you all the way," he assured me.

I thanked him.

"I've seen every fight," he told me. "And I think you're great."

I thought, *I see a lot of your commercials, and I think*—but what I said was, "Thanks, Jimmy." Again. I couldn't afford to be a bastard. I wanted him along with me. Someone on my side. More important, perhaps, someone who would still be on my side after the fight.

When the bell rang to end the fifteenth, or one of us was counted out, I knew I'd be alone. The proprietary interests would end there and then. If I won, it would be easy enough to find new ones. But win or lose, there'd always be Jimmy.

Valerian had a new suit, too. It almost seemed as if everyone had, except me. But it was a public occasion, and people always like to parade their newness on big nights. They like to show that they're at home in the wonderful disposable society, and that they have new clothes, new character, new feelings to replace the ones which went out with yesterday's garbage.

The old man didn't want to talk to me, but he couldn't help needing to look at me—to drink in my appearance and reinforce the idea that I was *his* instrument, the thunderbolt with which, from his Olympian heights, he was about to strike Herrera down.

"I want you to remember," I told him, "that I don't want you to get the least satisfaction out of this. I'm going into the ring the way I always have, to fight and win without any malice or emotion. I'm going to turn on a display of calculated, skillful boxing and I'm going to beat Herrera crisply and cleanly. You can suck at my mind for every instant of the fight, but you'll get absolutely nothing in the way of sadistic pleasure or vengeful fury out of me. You'll have to do your own fighting there."

It was a poor speech, but I was under strain. I tried to put it right, and I didn't, but I think the message was clear—maybe just a little too obvious.

I only hoped that I was right, and that I could keep it all down, where it belonged—submerged in my unconscious mind. Under constraint.

Valerian, of course, didn't try to argue with me. I don't think he even took exception to what I'd said. He just looked at me, memorizing my face because he'd never see me again.

While they were putting me into the sim there was a real crowd clustered round, each member of it with nothing to do and nothing to say, but each with some personal reason for wanting to be close, wanting to be involved. Some of them, I'd never even seen before.

Maria was there, silver hair still perfect, eyes steady, wearing an aura of perfect confidence. She had it all taped, all worked out according to theory. She was the only one who really knew the result in advance. We all had our doubts except her.

Curman was around, just hovering on the periphery, taking it all as it came along. For a moment or two, when my eye caught his and he winked, I envied the ease with which he coordinated himself. He was at peace with the alien world, and it didn't much matter to him which way the fight came out.

Ray Angeli was there, with the supply of advice finally dried up, the need to participate wavering at the last moment as he rediscovered uncertainty.

I hadn't seen Paul Herrera in the flesh. It's not Network policy for fighters to meet. I probably never would see him in the flesh this time, and I'd always have to remember him as a youth, an adolescent barbarian. I wondered, briefly, what he did look like now. But I didn't really want to know. I'd see his face in the sim. *The* face. The only one that mattered.

I closed my eyes before they masked me, and the world— crowds and all—went away into some hidden fold in space, some other dimension, some ridiculous dreamland. I didn't open them again until I was sure I'd open up on reality.

The ring.

I watched his presence bring the black body to life. I listened to the ghost voice chanting ritual in my ear. Somehow, I could feel the vamps settling in a vast cloud upon the colored air. I could sense the whole world turning on.

Time crept while nothing was happening inside. Outside—in that great imaginary complex in never-never-land called Network—the product was being carefully wrapped up. There were proprieties to be observed, formulae to be followed, visual cues to be manipulated, anticipations to be nurtured.

In the ring, it was all waiting.

Crippled time, shambling by.

I was alive and alone. I just went numb inside, waiting for it all to end. And begin.

We moved, and walked to face one another in the center of the ring, touching gloves, with faces showing nothing, because we were not yet wholly there.

Then the bell rang.

There were no preliminaries. There was to be no period of acclimatization, no wary trading of exploratory punches, no quiet settling into a languid prelude to a long crescendo. Herrera came out to reach me, to put in hard punches that would rattle me, that would count on the tally. He was aware, perhaps for the first time in years, of a possibility that be might be beaten, and he was hurrying to lay the ghost.

Maybe that was half the fight. Maybe before we even psyched into the ring I had him halfway down. But he intended to come all the way up again in no time at all. He attacked like a tiger.

I knew all about his speed, and as the jab came in I was watching for every little move that meant he was setting himself up for something bigger, something harder. I was always ready. I slid sideways, economically, always away from his driving right. I pushed forward with my left every time he overreached a fraction, pushing him out of his aggressive stance, making him pay for his hurry.

Hard punches were exchanged in the first minute. The first round filled up with action well before the bell and the vamps must have known early that we were both ready to bring it to a head well before the end. It was to be a real test, fast and hard.

The first finished even.

As the seconds of rest and recovery ticked away I was reaching inside myself, testing my state of mind, wanting to be neat and tidy, undisturbed. I felt, if anything, more detached than usual. I felt like a piece of clockwork mechanism, locked into a precise sequence of actions, moving with dour, uncaring efficiency.

I didn't just feel steady, I felt hardly alive. A zombie.

And so it went in the second. He came out to get me again and I let him come. I coped, with a strange easiness that was almost worrying. He was always searching for an opening, forcing his speed and insistent in his probing. But he couldn't find a thing. There was nothing for him. His punches were deflected by my arms, or barely connected with my body. I put in two good counterpunches. I won the round. It wasn't by much, but we both knew I had it.

Again, in the third, it was the same stand-up fight. We hardly clinched at all, we both wanted to stand back and throw what we could. And I was a shade the better. The pressure, for the moment, was on him.

In the fourth, the action congealed slightly as he began to reappraise the situation. His lips formed half-words, moving silently in tune with the thoughts firing the mind behind the face. All I could see was the rhythm in the words, I couldn't read the thoughts themselves. The lips were echoing some mental prayer—not a prayer to any personal God but to the pattern of reality which made him what he was. He was threatening me, talking at me, wishing me to death. He wanted to destroy me. It was a ritual, something that had become superimposed on his boxing in late years. He was conjuring up the ghost of Franco Valerian, using the strength he had stolen from that victory.

And it wasn't working. Again, I took the round. Just by a

fraction, but a fraction is enough—if you can keep the margin the same way.

And from the faint muscular distortion which tells you that a sim is being worn his features gradually changed. The eyes seemed to be kindled, and the fire of personality took hold of the face, lighting it. It was only a matter of time before it was the face. The trigger.

In the fifth he found me for the first time with a hard right, and I rocked. He hadn't got any faster, and I hadn't slowed down, but for once the probability went his way. He was very quick to try and capitalize on the break, and he hustled me with a new assurance, a new determination. He won the round, and all of a sudden my edge seemed very thin indeed, thin and ephemeral.

I was threatened, and I made bigger demands on my resources. I hurt him with a couple of right hooks, but didn't shake him. And anyhow, in the sixth I began to forget about the points. It didn't matter which of us was ahead on the tally. The tally hadn't got the whole story, or even a part of it. One of us was going to turn superhuman, and the other was going to crack. That's the way we'd both planned it.

Throughout the sixth it was all wrong. He was jabbing furiously, trying to batter down my defense, trying to clear a way through to the heart of me. I was still stalemating him, using up the time, but I wasn't making any difference to what was really going on. I was letting him call the tune, and I couldn't afford to leave it like that. I had to assert my own personality, put my stamp on the fight, so that while our strength was eroded and sapped into the machine along the carefully computed fatigue-gradient I could retain control. I had to think ahead, to the dying rounds when our skills would be threatened by the draining power, to the time when it would become desperate. I knew what Paul Herrera would have going for him then, but I was not at all sure what would be working for me.

Maybe Maria's seeds of hate would flower. But maybe not. Maybe I'd find something of my own.

In the few moments between rounds, I began to think about

failure. They say it's something you should never do, but I've never found that the things "they" say are as wise as "they" think. It's the logic of the masses, applicable in general but never in particular. I thought about failure, and wondered who was failing who, and if—

I knew by then that even now, I didn't hate Herrera. I wasn't horrified by him, or disgusted by him. In a sense, I knew him too well. I knew all about him, and I understood. I understood him better than Valerian, far better than the multitude of other people who'd barely impinged upon my life. Stella, Maria, Jimmy—they were shadows beyond the ring. But Paul was central. I knew Paul Herrera far too well.

As we came out for the seventh, the face was there, in all its crazy glory. Anguish and rage, tearing the false face apart. I looked into his eyes, and nothing stirred. No flood tide of emotion. There was nothing of Franco Valerian in me. None of it had taken. The graft had been too alien, and my mind had rejected it.

Maria had failed.

And he came at me with everything he had to throw. I tried to drive a hard right into his ribs—a blow to weaken him and take some of the lightning out of his motion—but he made it ineffective with a swerve and hooked his left into the temple above my right eye. The flesh swelled, and it hurt. The brain inside the sim's head was staggered. My mind, momentarily, was shaken and sickened.

I went into retreat. I sheltered from a rain of blows. I ran, I dodged, and finally I clinched, trying to hold him, trying to recover composure. I wanted to hold hard but when the voice says "Break", you break. You don't have the option.

I escaped, I overcame the lapse. On the tally I was probably still winning, but I knew that the only exchange which mattered now was the next one. What had gone before counted for nothing. The crisis was coming fast.

Again, the rest between rounds. Again, the thoughts crowding my mind. All the wrong thoughts, or so they say. I could hear a chorus building—a chorus singing, "I told you so". Not Stella this time but all of them. They'd tried to make me into their kind of toy and failed, but that wouldn't be *their* failure—not the way they'd write the script. This would be down to me. It would be *my* failure, my shit-out.

Then the change of state, which perhaps I needed desperately, happened inside my mind.

I became ultra-conscious of a presence—a presence I'd somehow forgotten, pushed deep in my mind during the early rounds. I became conscious of the people in my mind, with a new kind of awareness. They were there, suddenly, with a stark extrasensory clarity that made me wonder how I'd never seemed to notice them before.

It was the eighth, and somehow I carried in that round knowledge which had evaded me in the first seven. I could feel the millions of minds that were riding mine. I could feel their closeness, and it suddenly seemed very offensive.

I could smell them.

And I reacted against them.

I went cold. Completely cold. And I went out to mow down Paul Herrera with the same detachment and indifference and fatalism that a scythe might feel as it goes through ripe corn. I was sheer efficiency again, as crisp as I'd been in the first. Herrera had come to find me out, expecting to catch me weakening, giving way. From his point of view, time must have turned back. And with time, the tide of the fight. All the work he had put in suddenly showed for nothing, and that was something new to him. It was something he hadn't met before. He was used to wearing fighters down. They always pulled out extra, always lasted longer than they showed likely to—but they always wore on. They never turned back and came again. Not this way.

He sensed the change, knew the difference. He was as aware of it as I was. We fought out the round, and from the ringside we must both have looked like champions. Great fighters. But through the E-links, I knew—we both knew—that we didn't seem the same at all. As different as black and white, dead and alive, high and low. He was a blaze of glory, I was a black, cold knife.

There was no possibility of a standoff. One of us had to win, and win utterly. He was feeding the vamps, pouring himself into their heads. I was walling them off, fighting them, maybe even hating them.

The riders—the riders I couldn't satisfy, who wanted from me a tribute I could not and would not pay them—became the focus of my mental force. And with them—inextricably enmeshed with them—their figurehead, their beloved, their prime victim, Paul Herrera.

We came out for the ninth both knowing that he was losing, that fate had changed hands. He came at me full of the compulsion to force the critical moment he already knew must go against him. He attacked, with all the venom that was still in him.

And as his fury mounted beyond effect, so my calm settled over me like a cloak.

The first blow, when I breached a gap in his guard as he tried to hook at my eyes, was a solid one—the best punch of the fight. It should have rocked him and thrown him back, but it didn't. It brought him on, more determined, more furious than before.

There's a fable about an adder which struck at a file, and was hurt. Instead of the hurt making it desist, it only made the adder strike again, and again and again and again, the agony of each strike driving the compulsion to strike again harder, in a positive feedback loop that could only be broken by the death and destruction of the snake.

And that's how it went.

Herrera shed his skill, his speed—everything but his fists and his need to keep them flying. His defense evaporated, and it became so much easier to hit him. I couldn't miss.

With ten, a dozen, a score of punches driven into his face and body in a matter of four, six, eight seconds, the legend of Paul Herrera exploded—tested, at last, beyond his capabilities.

He should have gone down long before he did, but something

kept him standing, left him stranded in the middle of the ring to soak up the punishment. Twenty years of winning and hurting all turned back on Herrera then, and perhaps he had to unlive them all before he fell.

I did it without anger in my mind. There was blood on my gloves but none on my hands, no stain on my soul. I had no sense of triumph. I simply knew that in beating Herrera I was beating the mind-vampires—the real killers of Franco Valerian.

You don't hear cheers inside a sim.

After you win, you're all alone.

Until—

CHAPTER FOURTEEN

A world was waiting for me—an artificial world ruled by the mythology of victory and acclamation. Into that world I had been reborn. I could never be no one again—not until the moment comes when I, like Paul Herrera, will end up as the wreckage of a defeated sim.

With the electrodes stripped away, the knowledge that I had beaten Herrera retreated reluctantly into the past, and I faced the future. There was a clamoring crowd of new thoughts, new ideas. In a way that made me want to laugh, I believed that I had beaten them all, robbed them of their petty triumphs.

And I did laugh.

"Where's Valerian?" I demanded. "I want to know what he got for his money."

Maria was there, with the techs. She stepped forward to take the question.

"He got what he wanted," she said. She looked calm and composed, not angry. "You won't be hearing from him again," she added. "You're on your own now."

"He didn't get what he wanted," I retorted. "I didn't do it his way. Nor your way. My head was straight."

She smiled, and there was a gleam in the smile that mocked me.

"He was hooked into Herrera," she said.

The last surprise. The last trick. They had it saved up. In a way, it was still funny, though it didn't make me laugh. Of course he was hooked up to Herrera. It was obvious. In eighteen years, he had always been hooked to Herrera. Crossed connections, for a different angle. He had got what he wanted—not out of my empty head but out of Herrera's. He had seen Herrera beaten, and sucked up his suffering. Herrera—the greatest feeler of them all—must have gone out in a real blaze of agony. A real freak-out.

"And you?" I said. "Whose head were you on?"

"Yours," she said. That gleam was still there. She wasn't about to give in.

"And?" I prompted.

"You won," she said.

"Not according to the script."

"I don't write scripts," she said. "I make pens, for people to write their own."

"You think you can claim responsibility for what I did tonight?"

She shook her head. "I never claim responsibility. I just do what I can and watch the results. I'm still watching, and I'll go on watching. You have to go into the ring again and again and again, because that's the way you want your life to run. Every time, you'll take those people inside you, and you'll make power out of hating what they are. It'll win your fights, and it'll tear you apart. You come back in ten years and you tell me whether I taught you anything or not."

"Stella's right," I said. "You're a real bitch."

"What does that make you?" she asked, sweetly. "An electric hare?"

I was grateful that she'd had to say that. I was pleased to find a hole, however small, in her quiet arrogance.

"I'm the champion," I told her. "The best man. The winner."

"And they'll hate you for it," she reminded me. "They'll detest your callousness and your lack of feeling. But in time, they'll find that they love to hate you. They'll ride you like Valerian rode Herrera—looking to see you broken up and destroyed. And when the time comes they'll dance on your grave. You can't beat the public—not in the long run. They'll get their kicks out of you no matter what you try to peddle them."

And that little speech replaced, "Goodbye." She left. It was the end of a beautiful relationship.

Outside, Jimmy was waiting for me, waiting to claim his slice of my reflected glory. We were both big men, now—with the world opening its doors for us.

He was all smiles. He'd been hooked up to me, and he hadn't resented the way I'd done it. He probably hadn't even noticed. What the hell did he need with an E-link? He'd done all the feeling himself—he'd felt my victory like nobody else, his way.

He shook me by the hand, and every inch of him believed it when he said, "You—*did* it."

"Sure," I said, shaking his hand as hard as he was shaking mine, "I sure as hell *did.*"

Then I went out, to find a new home within my new life.

ABOUT THE AUTHOR

Brian Stableford was born in Yorkshire in 1948. He taught at the University of Reading for several years, but is now a full-time writer. He has written many science-fiction and fantasy novels, including *The Empire of Fear*, *The Werewolves of London*, *Year Zero*, *The Curse of the Coral Bride*, *The Stones of Camelot*, and *Prelude to Eternity*. Collections of his short stories include a long series of *Tales of the Biotech Revolution*, and such idiosyncratic items as *Sheena and Other Gothic Tales* and *The Innsmouth Heritage and Other Sequels*. He has written numerous nonfiction books, including *Scientific Romance in Britain, 1890-1950*; *Glorious Perversity: The Decline and Fall of Literary Decadence*; *Science Fact and Science Fiction: An Encyclopedia*; and *The Devil's Party: A Brief History of Satanic Abuse*. He has contributed hundreds of biographical and critical articles to reference books, and has also translated numerous novels from the French language, including books by Paul Féval, Albert Robida, Maurice Renard, and J. H. Rosny the Elder.